I0587802

Robert Starnes

An Exciting and Adventurous way to view History

Book Five of the

Saving History Series

Final

Hour

Robert Starnes

Robert Starnes

Published by Starnes Books LLC
Edited by Carpenter Editing Services, LLC

ISBN: 978-1-7347928-7-4 (sc)
ISBN: 978-1-7347928-8-1 (e)
ISBN: 978-1-7347928-9-8 (hc)

Library of Congress Control Number: 2020924625

Printed in the United States of America
First Printing 2020

Dedication

I want to take the time to dedicate this final installment of the *Saving History Series, Final Hour*, to any and everyone who has been affected by the Coronavirus (SARS-CoV-2) or COVID-19.

There have been so many lives lost just in 2020 alone due to this pandemic of COVID-19. Nothing can bring them back, but we will never forget them. This virus strikes without prejudice or discrimination. No one suffers the same way, and hardly anyone has the same symptoms, which makes this year 2020 a year in History. Thank you to all the "essential workers" who had to work during such a horrible time in History.

I am proud to be part of several COVID-19 survivor groups on Facebook, because as a two-time survivor myself, I still need support. There is nothing wrong with getting help from others going through what you are when others may not believe you. This pandemic has also increased anxiety, depression, and suicide in the United States. I want everyone to know you are not in this alone.

Please seek help in any way possible via the suicide hotline at 1-800-273-8255. If you are feeling depressed or anxious, see your Dr. as soon as possible. Please don't give up hope.

We know that wearing a mask or even participating in social distancing does not stop the COVID-19 pandemic, but it does reduce the chances of catching it. Remember, just because you may not believe in safety precautions for COVID-19, at least do it for the others who do believe in their safety as well as yours.

For those who do not know about Pandora's Box, it is in Greek Mythology about how Zeus sent Pandora down to earth to marry Epimetheus. His brother, Prometheus, warned Zeus how to defeat the Titans. For this information, Zeus gave them both special powers. Due to their loyalty to Zeus, he gave them both the power to create the first creatures on earth. Epimetheus created each animal and gave them special skills and a form of protection. Prometheus took his time to mold man but was left with no forms of protection since Epimetheus had already given them all away. Prometheus went against Zeus' orders and gave man fire for protection and was punished by Zeus.

Since Prometheus made men and went against Zeus, to punish men, Zeus created a woman named Pandora. She was molded to look like the goddess Aphrodite and received the gifts of wisdom, beauty, kindness, peace, generosity, and health from the gods.

As a wedding present, Zeus gave Pandora a box but warned her never to open it. Since she was created to be curious, she couldn't stay away from the box and opened it. Once she did, horrible things flew out of the box including, greed, envy, hatred, pain, disease, hunger, poverty, war, and death. Since all the miseries had been let out of Pandora's box, the only thing that did not make it out was HOPE! Since then, people have been able to hold on to that hope to survive the wickedness of the box Pandora let out. It keeps them going.

I say this to remind you all that there is hope at the end of every tunnel and also left in Pandora's box, so never give up. There is still HOPE!

Robert Starnes

Contents

Prologue: Travis the Fixer?

"And where do you think you are going? You cannot create the greatest possible mess in history, then just walk out and leave the rest of us to wait to see if what you have done was the right or wrong thing to do," the Council Leader billows to King Payton before he walks out of the Council meeting room.

"Do not think that just because my brother is gone that you can speak to me in any way you want. It would serve you to remember that I am a King. Not just any King, but the King of the Embers. So, if you enjoy our world as it is now, then back off," King Payton demands.

With those final words from the King, the remaining High Leaders, Fisher and Emma, along with the Council Leader, allowed King Payton to leave the room. The room remained silent until Travis of the Windairians walked back into the meeting room. As he enters, all heads turn in disbelief. They all know that Travis was excused from the group for not being able to help out with time travel. Obviously, that was not the truth, or they would not be back here now. They can help with time travel.

Travis walks into the room, walks directly over to his spot he once occupied at the Council table, and takes a seat. "What's the matter with you all? You act as if you are seeing a ghost."

"I'm sorry, Travis, but you have already claimed that you have no idea of what we need from your people, and because of that, you have been dismissed. This is not the type of meeting where you can just come back when you want. Our circumstances have not changed; therefore, you are still not needed unless your abilities have changed. Have they?" the Council Leader asks Travis bluntly.

"You might say that they have. Let's say that we, with my help, are going to be able to help some of the things you all messed up in the past so far. Trust me when I say you are going to need our help before this is even close to being corrected," Travis defines his current abilities.

About the time Travis finishes, King Payton walks back into the Council meeting room. "What's he doing here?" he asks while pointing at Travis.

"Claiming he can fix what we have done to the past, but we are all assuming he is talking about what you have done most of all," Rose explains to King Payton.

"How dare you speak to me in that way…"

"I'm sorry to cut you off, King Payton, but we don't have any time for your threats of 'how dare you' right now. If you could please take your seat and let me get started, I will show you all what you all have done wrong," Travis instructs the King, as he follows his instruction and takes his seat.

"Now, can I begin?" Travis asks the group.

Chapter 1

Garrett's Mind?

"And how can you help me? Do you know the location of Kayla, Brayden, Connor, and Maria?" Junior asks Garrett's mind he's now occupying.

"Actually, I do. I know because I am here with them. I have been with your two friends since they arrived, and I can assure you they have not been harmed," Garrett replies to Junior.

"Great, then tell me where you are so I can tell Ian and Kenzie. That way we can go there, where you are now, and help you rescue all of them, except Maria, that is," Junior demands.

"Wait a second there, Junior. I can't tell you where we are right now because it will put all of us in danger. We have to let Brayden continue trying to get into Kayla's mind. Brayden will be able to lie to Mason about what he sees. That will be the only way to get Mason to stop trying this and start trusting Kayla more. Do you understand?" Garrett asks Junior.

"Not in the least. I don't know why it is so important for Mason to trust Kayla when Ian and his friends are willing to come and rescue them all, including Kayla," Junior spits back to Garrett.

"Junior, there is more riding on this mission than just a rescue. History is at stake here. You can't come and just save everyone, we have to make a difference. If Ian and Kenzie come and just save everyone, then this will be the history that remains. And it will be repeated again and again, unless we change Mason's outlook on life, or just in general. Do you understand how important this mission is, for the future?" Garrett pleads with Junior.

"How do you know so much about the future? Are you from the future?" Junior asks Garrett.

"I don't see how any of that information can help us now, do you? Speaking of the future, why is it that I can't feel a body attached to your mind?" Garrett digs deeper with Junior.

"Excuse me? You said that before. How can you tell if I have a body or not? I can promise you that I most certainly do have a body!"

"Let's say I have special gifts like the others here, and this is one of mine. You say you have a body, but it can't be in this time period; therefore, you are from the future or the past. Which now leads me to some questions, like what are you doing here now? What do you hope to change, and who are you going to have to use to achieve your goals?"

"I'm sorry, but we do not have time for such questions. I am, somehow here, in your mind, while you are awake, that has to mean something. You know your location, and I need it, so you can at least give me your location. If you think I should wait before telling Ian and Kenzie, I will wait, but at least tell me. This way, if anything happens to you, I will be able to tell the others where you are before anyone else gets hurt."

"As long as you don't divulge our location until I tell you, then it's okay. Do you understand what I am saying, and do you agree?"

"Yes, I understand and promise to follow your instructions."

"Then I will show you our location, but I can't stress enough how important it is that you wait until I tell you it's okay to hurry up and get here. Please, you have to understand that. All of our future lives depend on you waiting to tell Ian and the others."

"Yes, I said, I promise. I will not give anyone your location until you tell me it's all right. Now that I have been inside your mind, if you need me, all you have to do is think of me when you need my help. I will feel that and will be able to come back anytime I'm needed."

With that, Garrett shows their location with Junior's mind, but as soon as he does, he has to ask Junior to leave because Mason is not happy with the outcome from Brayden's work. "Junior, I'm sorry, but it's time you left. Mason is not very happy right now and wants all of our full attention. Please, go back to Ian and Kayla and let them know that everything is fine for now. But if things get bad, you will be able to lead them here, and only then. Understand?"

"Yes, Garrett, I completely understand, and I will not say anything about your location unless you ask me," are the last words Junior says to Garrett before he is removed from his mind.

***

As Garrett has lost the connection with Junior with his mind, he is able to listen to what Mason is saying. He is upset that Brayden has been unable to penetrate Kayla's mind. Brayden has been unable to dream-walk Kayla because of a Kelly song, 'Broken Pieces,' which kept playing extremely loud in Kayla's mind. This caused Brayden to not be able to enter Kayla's mind. All Brayden could hear was the song repeating, over and over again in Kayla's mind without being able to go any further into Kayla's memories. They are calling it some kind of defense spell that was put in Kayla's mind by someone else.

"Well, Mason, who could have put such a strange defense spell on Kayla's mind?" Maria asks.

"There is only one person I can think of, but if it is true, then that means we have a lot more problems to worry about than just Kayla's mind being blocked," Mason responds.

"What do you mean? And who do you think it could be that has placed this block on her mind?" Maria questions Mason.

"That is not a topic we should get into right now. Right now, we need Brayden to try again to dream-walk Kayla," Mason explains. "Are you able and ready to try again to dream-walk Kayla?" Mason asks Brayden.

"Yes, I can try again. Now that I know what I am up against, I may be able to force myself past that barrier. Let's just hope that this is the only barrier that has been placed on Kayla's mind, or this could be a very long process," Brayden informs the room.

"Then it's time to lie back down and face the music. Do you think you can handle her music?" Mason asks somewhat jokingly.

"We are about to find out," Brayden answers while lying back on the bed again. As Brayden closes his eyes and begins to breach Kayla's mind, so he can try and dream-walk her again, he is met with the song, 'Broken Pieces,' blearing in Kayla's mind again. Brayden decides to take a different approach this time. Brayden begins to sing along with the song in a very loud voice. To his surprise, the song stops playing in Kayla's mind. Now Brayden is able to move past the exterior of Kayla's mind.

Brayden takes this opportunity to go deeper into Kayla's mind to see what she is dreaming about. He knows it may be something he will have to lie about to Mason, but Brayden also knows he has to go into Kayla's dreams at one point or another.

As Brayden moves deeper into Kayla's mind, the clearer things become. Now what he sees is not exactly what he is expecting. Brayden can see a small girl in the middle of a room, and he believes it to be Kayla. She is sitting in the middle of a room filled with puzzle pieces. She is not working on any puzzle that Brayden can tell. She is just sitting in the middle of a room of puzzle pieces.

"Kayla? Do you remember me? Do you know who I am? It's me, Brayden, a friend of Ian's. I am here because Mason expects me to go back and tell him any secrets you may be hiding from him, but you don't have to worry about that. I am not going to tell Mason anything that he wants to know. I will only tell him what we want him to think, you know. Can you turn around and talk to me, Kayla?" Brayden asks the little girl, sitting in the middle of the room of puzzle pieces with her back turned to him.

Brayden begins to move closer to the little girl, but before he is able to make it to her, she turns around and tells him to stop.

"Please, don't come any closer to me. You are stepping on all the pieces, and if you damage them, they won't be able to be put back together in the future. Is that why you are here? Has my father sent you here to make sure I stay broken forever?" the young girl asks the stranger to her, Brayden.

"I'm sorry. I thought you were a friend of mine, Kayla. But I can see that you aren't, so what's your name? My name is Brayden, and no, your father did not send me here. I was only sent here to find my friend, Kayla. I would never come here to try to make someone stay broken forever. I would actually want to help. Is there anything I can do for you to help you while I look for my friend? I would hate to know that you are out here, somewhere, feeling like you are broken, because I can assure you, you are not broken. You are a special piece of a puzzle that is just waiting for the perfect puzzle to fit in for the rest of your life. I promise."

"Well, Brayden, my name is Kelly, and I don't know your friend, Kayla. I do know that if you don't stop moving around, you will destroy my chances of ever being put back together. I am supposed to be put back together, piece by piece, by someone who will restore my faith that a man can be kind and a father can stay. So, please stop destroying my chances of happiness," Kelly tells Brayden.

Kelly is sitting in a room full of puzzle pieces, and the song that was playing was 'Broken Pieces' by an American singer. *What are the chances that this is a younger version of that young singer, and this is another block in Kayla's mind?* Brayden wonders to himself.

"Where are we, Kelly? And what's your last name?" Brayden asks of Kelly.

"I'm not sure where we are. I have been here for so long, waiting to be who I am meant to be. And my full name is just Kelly. Why do you want to know?"

"I am just wanting to get a full grasp of where I am and whose mind I may be in. Are we in your mind, or are you a memory put inside of Kayla's mind?"

"I'm sorry, but I don't know what you're talking about. I'm going to have to ask you to leave my room now, so I can wait for HIM to show up and put me back together because of all of the broken pieces HE has left. So, if you don't mind, this is goodbye," Kelly tells Brayden, and as she does, he is pulled out of Kelly's room and all the way back out to the sound of the song 'Broken Pieces' by the little girl he just left Kelly. The song is still so loud he breaks his connection with Kayla and wakes up in the bed in the room next to Kayla's room.

"What's wrong now, Brayden?" Mason asks.

"I think it is another block in Kayla's mind. I made it past the loud music barrier, but this time I was transported to a room with a small girl in it. I assumed it was Kayla at first, but then I was corrected. The room was full of puzzle pieces, and the small girl was sitting in the middle of the room. As I moved closer to her, after she did not answer my questions of who she was, she turned and stopped me from moving forward. She said I was damaging the puzzle pieces and that someone is supposed to find them to put them back together. Then when I asked her what her name was, she said, 'Kelly.' I was seeing the inspiration behind the song that was playing in the outer part of the barrier, 'Broken Pieces,' by the adult version of Kelly. I could feel the pain she was feeling as she was writing the words and singing them for the first time. I could feel her sorrow as I stood in the room with all the puzzle pieces just waiting to be found and put back together, so she could feel whole and loved again. Then she made me leave, and I ended up in the part of Kayla's mind that actually was playing the song, 'Broken Pieces,' so loud that I had to break my connection with Kayla's mind," Brayden finishes.

"So, what you are telling us is that you still have not been able to dream-walk Kayla?" Mason states to Brayden.

"No, what I am telling you is that there are several levels of protection around Kayla's mind. After the music, which I was able to get past, is another layer of protection. It's a room with a young Kelly sitting on the floor of a room full of puzzle pieces, but now I have to figure out how to pass this one. I am not going to be able to crack through, however many blocks she has in her mind, tonight. I can assure you that. Those spells are strong, and each one requires more of my energy, which I am running low on right now," Brayden replies back to Mason.

As Brayden finishes, Mason begins to pace the floor of the bedroom they have been using. He is not saying a word, but he has a look of distrust on his face. Maria is not sure if Brayden is telling the truth or not, and that has her very worried.

"Is there anything you are leaving out? Something you don't want to tell me?" Mason finally speaks, breaking the silence to ask Brayden a few follow up questions.

"I have left nothing out. Everything I know about the inside of Kayla's mind, you know as well. Why would I want to hold anything from you? The sooner I do this for you, the sooner Connor and I can leave this place. So, trust me when I say, you will know what I know when I know it. And if I thought I could finish it right now, I would do it, so we should leave. The last thing I want is for Connor or me to stay here any longer than we have to," Brayden snaps back to Mason.

If Mason had doubts before about Brayden's loyalties, they are all gone now. Mason has never had someone speak to him in that tone. He decides to let the matter pass, because he still needs Brayden. "Fine. Why don't we call it a night for their first try then? Garrett, Maclaine, will you two escort our guests down to their quarters in the basement cells, so they can get plenty of rest without being disturbed. Maria, you are welcome to use this room if you like. I am going to head to my office for a little bit of work before bed, then tomorrow evening, we will start right back up where we left off, right here in this room. Is that understood?" Mason asks everyone.

With a quick nod from everyone, they all go their separate ways for the evening.

***

"You can come out now, Kayla. He's gone."

"Are you sure he's gone?"

"Yes, I'm sure. Now come out here."

Kayla comes sneaking out from behind a piece of white wall that is undetectable by the naked eye. She makes her way over to Kelly, who is still sitting on the floor.

"I don't know how I can ever thank you enough for helping me. To be honest, I'm still not sure why you agreed to do this in the first place," Kayla comments to Kelly.

"Let's say that I owe a debt to Alexis, and she told me that one day she would ask for my help, and me helping her in the future is all she wanted for helping me at my present time. Plus, it was kind of fun playing a creepy little me, sitting in a room full of puzzle pieces," Kelly confesses.

"Do you believe him? About Mason wanting to find things out about me, but that he is not going to tell Mason what he finds out?" Kayla asks Kelly one last question.

"I do believe him. I felt his emotions and intentions, and they were genuine. Whatever they have planned, they are trying to fill you in about it, without Mason knowing. The next time he comes in, and he will be back, you should let him in and see what he has to say. I mean, what could it hurt?" Kelly finishes as she turns and walks towards one of the white walls, unseen by the naked eye, and slides behind it, and she is gone.

Chapter 2

Chad?

Mason does not have any real work to do in his office before bed. He is just not ready for bed yet. He does, however, have plenty of things to think about and none of them are very pleasant. He would rather do some paperwork instead.

Just as Mason enters his office, he is visited by a body guest he has encountered previously. "What are you doing? You just let everyone go their own way and get some rest when you were so close to breaking into Kayla's mind. What type of fool are you?" Mason's body guest questions him out loud in his own voice.

"What are you talking about? We are no closer to breaking through Kayla's security walls than before we knew she had any. If you know so much about Kayla and how important it is for us to dream-walk her, why didn't you mention the security walls around her mind? That seems like something important that I should have been told so I could have prepared Brayden on what to expect," Mason replies to his inner guest.

"Why are you questioning me now? Everything I have told you has been the truth or has come true after the fact. You have not answered my question," Mason's inner guest retorts.

"And what question would that be?" Mason asks his body guest.

"What kind of fool are you? You know what? You don't have to answer that question as it was rhetorical in the first place. You have no idea just how important this is to me. I mean, to the future. We are running out of time, so you need to get them all back and keep trying to get into Kayla's mind," Mason's guest demands.

"First, I do things my way, so you can stop trying to order me around. Second, I would not believe much more of what you tell me. You have already slipped and given it away that whatever this is that you are so determined for us to do, is only to benefit you. And finally, I will not do another thing you ask, or try to demand, until you tell me your name," Mason puts his foot down, making his demands very clear to his guest.

"I don't understand what my name has to do with what you need to do, but if you insist, my name is Chad. Now, is knowing my name going to assist you in completing the task at hand?"

"Not in the least bit, but it does take away some of the power you thought you had over me, wouldn't you say? You are no longer a complete mystery. Now, if you don't back off and let me do things my way, I will find a way to research you, and you will become MY mission. So again, do I make myself clear, Chad?"

"Mason, there are things about me that you can't even imagine. One example is that if I want, I can simply take over control of your body and do exactly what I want, while you would be sitting in the back of your own mind, only being able to watch. You see, where I am from, we are way more advanced than you and your people are. So the next time you feel the need to snap back at me, remember what I just told you. Do I make myself clear?"

Before Mason has a chance to answer Chad, his own hand swings up and slaps his own face. It wasn't Mason who slapped him but Chad showing he means business with his threats of taking over Mason's body.

"Yes, you have made yourself very clear. Now, if you don't mind, I have some things I need to attend to before getting some rest myself, and I would rather be alone."

"Fine, have it your way for tonight, but tomorrow you had better show some results. If you don't, I just might have to take over for myself," are the last words from Chad before leaving Mason's body for the evening.

Now that Mason is alone, he heads over to his safe. As he moves closer and closer towards his destination, he keeps thinking of just how close he is to the possibility of having his family back. Even though he does not remember a life with them, it is that thought alone that fuels his drive to keep going at all costs. That is also what makes Mason so dangerous. The lines between right and wrong are buried in Mason, or he simply does not care. He only cares about what he wants, much like Chad does, both not thinking anything about the consequences it could cause to everyone else in the world.

Mason stops in front of his safe, presses the code, and once the light turns green, he turns the handle to open the safe door. Once the door is pulled completely open, Mason reaches in and pulls out the photo of the family he believes should be his but was taken away by Sebastian, with his excessive use of the Time Keeper. Sebastian used the Time Keeper so many times to keep his and his best friend Grayson's friendship intact, causing so many time ripples, they erased his family one by one. At least, this is what Mason has concluded. Holding the photo, Mason thinks, *Soon, we will all be together again.* Then Mason places the photo back into the safe. He shuts and locks the safe door and turns to make his way to his office door. After his conversation with Chad, he is feeling a bit more tired than he was earlier. So Mason decides to go to his room earlier than expected. Mason grabs his office door handle, gives it a turn, and pulls his door open. As the door is open, Mason steps into the hall, closes his door, and begins his walk down to his sleeping quarters.

***

Once everyone is asked to leave and they go to their rooms, Garrett and Maclaine are ordered to take Brayden and Connor back down to the basement. On their way to the elevators, Garrett asks Maclaine if he doesn't mind taking them down by himself, saying he has something he needs to take care of before he goes to his room. Maclaine says he is fine with that.

Once Maclaine, and the others, were tucked in the elevator and headed down to the basement,

Garrett decides to follow Mason to wherever he is headed. Garrett still has suspicions about Mason and his true motives. Garrett is able to follow Mason to his office undetected.

Once Mason enters his office and closes his door, Garrett is able to come out of the shadows and stand next to Mason's office door. He takes a position where he can see down both directions of the hallway, just in case any of Mason's real guards come towards him. He wants to make sure he is not interrupted as he listens to Mason in his office.

It only takes a minute for Garrett to hear Mason's voice. He is not sure if someone else was already in the room waiting for Mason, so he decides to listen and see where the conversion leads. As soon as Garrett hears Mason questioning himself about letting everyone go their own way and sleep tonight, in his own voice, Garrett knows right then that Mason is not alone. He also knows Mason is the only person physically in the room.

I knew it! Mason has a visitor as well. Now I need to find out who is helping him and why, Garrett thinks to himself with great satisfaction. Garrett knows this all to be true after hearing Mason ask himself, "What type of fool are you?" about himself in his own voice.

Even as Garrett's suspicions are confirmed, he decides to wait outside of Mason's office door as long as he can. He is hoping that Mason's body guest will reveal who he is and why he is here now. Garrett is supposed to be the only student or person from his time and place sent here at this time. Anyone else will be in violation of not only the school rules but also the rules of time travel.

Garrett does not have to wait long outside Mason's office before he hears Mason's voice reveal the name of the person from Garrett's time and place. He hears Mason say his name is Chad, one of the biggest bullies in Garrett's school. The teachers tried everything with him. But, with all the outlandish laws in his time and place, the bullies have more rights than the teachers, parents, or even the victims of his bullying. The laws seem to protect the bully and be against anyone who would speak out against them. That includes their own parents.

Now that Garrett knows who is working against him, he pretty much understands why he is here. Chad is the type of person that will not give up until he feels he has destroyed his opponent. Garrett knows this because he has been through Chad's torments for most of his school years. Chad not only bullies Garrett but almost every other smart student at their school. Chad's mission is to compromise all of the smart students' projects so they won't make the highest grades they possibly can or normally would. His bullying allows him to make his lower grades look right in line with all the others.

Garrett remains at Mason's office door to see just what other information Chad, or Mason, will reveal about their plans.

Little does Garrett know, he is about to get more than what he bargained for. Garrett gets to hear Mason argue with Chad, one trying to bully the other. Garrett finds it funny that his bully, Chad, has met his match in Mason. Garrett knows Mason is more than a very dangerous bully, and Chad is not ready for this.

Garrett lets Mason and Chad have their argument until it is over. He hears Mason tell Chad he made himself clear, then Garrett hears Mason tell Chad to have it his way tonight, but tomorrow better show some results.

Garrett does not hear any more arguments from Mason with himself, so he decides to make his way to his own room. He turns and begins his way down the hallway that leads to the front entry sitting area. Once through the sitting area, Garrett only has to head down the hallway that ends at his barrack door. The same door where he met Kayla for the first time, the time she was about to enter his room while he was exiting at the same time. That's when she began to fall forward, then Garrett caught her in his arms. Garrett gives a little smile to himself with just the thought of Kayla.

Arriving at his destination, Garrett reaches for his doorknob and gives it a slow turn as if he is waiting for Kayla to fall into his arms again. But the door just opens, no Kayla waiting for him on the other side this time. Garrett closes his door and walks over to his dresser. He reaches into his pocket and pulls out a puzzle piece, one single puzzle piece he has had since he began his assignment. He places it in a small box in the top drawer of the dresser. He was never told what the puzzle piece was for when it was given to him upon his arrival to begin his history assignment. He was only told that it would be one of the most important keys for a successful lesson.

Now that the puzzle piece is tucked safely away, Garrett begins to prepare for bed.

***

Ian, Kenzie, and Jax are talking through different things to see what they need to do next. They know they have somehow been given an extra forty-five minutes after they met with Junior in Ian's mind.

"So why do you think we have been given these extra minutes? There must be something we can do differently this time that will help us. At least this is the best I can come up with," Ian tells the others.

"Is there any way that you may have stored this memory in the Time Keeper, then accessed it with Kenzie still in your mind?" Jax asks Ian.

"I don't know, to be honest. I guess anything is possible," Ian replies.

"I don't believe it was you, Ian. I can tell you something happened to us, but it was not when we were asleep or not fully asleep anyway. Whatever happened to us happened as we were going to sleep the second time, causing it to be our first time. I think if Ian were to have stored that memory of our meeting with Junior in the Time Keeper, then we, or he, would have remembered the meeting. But the meeting has been erased from both of our memories. Do you have that kind of power, Ian?" Kenzie speaks up with some very sound and compelling evidence.

After Kenzie finishes with her thoughts on the matter, Jax and Ian have nothing to say at the moment. The pair need a few minutes to let Kenzie's brilliance settle into their minds.

"Kenzie, I am so glad you found me that day when you showed up out of nowhere and into the stairwell of Kayla and my apartment community in

Brooklyn. I think we will listen to your ideas about what to do next. You seem to be the only one that has a grasp on what is going on," Ian tells Kenzie, which she can tell he is speaking for Jax as well.

"I'm flattered, so thank you, but we will work on this together. We are a team," Kenzie tells them both. "Now, I do have something. Do you remember how we got out of Maria's room? Once we were back in your room, and Jax caught you coming down from talking to River Kate, Garrett took over your body, and you missed River Kate's party, by the way. I'm sure she will forgive you. Anyway, do you remember Garrett?"

"Of course, I remember him. That was not the first time he had taken over my body, but it is the first time he had introduced himself. What are you thinking, Kenzie?" Ian replies with a smile.

"Well, there were a lot of questions he would not, or could not, answer, but why? How could the fact that we know anything about him, or a mission he is on, put his mission in jeopardy? I think I have an answer to those questions."

"Let's hear the answers then. Don't leave us waiting," Jax speaks up.

"As you told me when Garrett was here in Ian's body, maybe I was drawn to that body. Also, what if he couldn't tell us anything about his mission because we are all on the same mission? Maybe the body Garrett was using is connected to Kayla, or maybe it was Kayla's body. He said he's been helping us, and he will continue to help us. That has to mean he is with Kayla, Brayden, Connor, and Maria," Kenzie finishes with a clap of her hands.

"Now I have to say that all makes perfect sense. Why else has he been helping us? I think I know why we were given those extra forty-five minutes now," Ian suggests.

"And just why do you think you were given that extra time?" Jax asks.

"Because the first time Garrett was here explaining how we made it out of Maria's room, we were not ready. We did not ask the right questions of Garrett. Now, if we can get Garrett to come back here to take over my body, to explain it again, we can ask him very different questions," Ian sounds pleased with his idea.

"There is also something else that you left out," Kenzie brings up another point.

"And what would that be?" Ian asks.

"I know how to find them now. If my pull was to the body Garrett was using, then I might be able to teleport to that body this time while I'm awake."

"That's right. But to be sure it's the body of someone we are trying to save, you should not try it yet. Garrett could have been using Mason's body for all we know. We can clarify with Garrett and with our new questions to make sure, and he will never know what we are planning," Ian finishes.

"I like it!" Kenzie shouts.

"I do as well, so let's make our way down to your room, Ian, since that is where Garrett comes to your rescue," Jax suggests to Ian and Kenzie.

The three of them make their way out of the Sky Lounge and take the stairs one flight down to Ian's floor to go to Brayden and his room to get ready for round two with Garrett.

Chapter 3

Early Morning?

Mason wakes up bright and early the next morning. He recalls his conversation with Chad, his body guest, from last night. Mason knows that he has got to get some results today. If he doesn't, then he's afraid Chad will follow through with what he threatened and take over Mason's body and do things his way instead. Mason already knows what Chad is capable of, and if he wants to take over Mason's body, he will.

With the thought of Chad taking over his body, Mason is going to make sure Brayden can breach Kayla's dreams this morning. Mason knows that Chad's reasons are not the same as his, and Chad will mess up any plans of Mason getting his family back. That is something that he will not allow to happen. No matter what he has to do at this point.

Mason gets up, out of bed, heads to the shower, and gets ready for this important day. It does not take Mason long to shower and get dressed for the day. He already has his clothes picked out and ready. After showering, Mason makes a call to Maria, who calls Maclaine, who calls Garrett, to all meet down in the basement cells where Brayden and Connor are still being held.

As everyone does as they were told, Mason waits another thirty minutes, so he can make sure that everyone is ready and down in the basement when he arrives.

Maria makes her way from her room and towards the elevators which will take her to the basement, as instructed. As she is walking down the hallway, she meets Maclaine.

"Have you seen Garrett yet?" Maria asks Maclaine.

"Not yet. You are the first person I have seen so far this early in the morning," replies a sleepy Maclaine.

"You did call Garrett after I called you, correct?" Maria asks Maclaine.

"Yes, I called him, and he said he would be there," Maclaine replies. "Do you know why Mason is so eager about us getting up this early?"

"All I know is that Mason is going to expect Brayden to do what he has to do to get into Kayla's mind, or I have a feeling he is going to use Connor to force her to let Brayden in. That is something that I will not allow to happen," Maria informs Maclaine.

"And just what do you suggest we do to keep such a thing like that from happening?"

"I'm not sure. We better come up with something quick, once we are down in the basement with Brayden and Connor before Mason makes his way down." Just as Maria finishes her last sentence, she and Maclaine find themselves standing in front of the elevators. Maria presses the call button, and they both wait.

*****

Garrett makes sure he wakes up extra early so that he can go down to the basement to have some alone time with Brayden and Connor. He wants to make sure they have a plan set in case Brayden is unable to break through Kayla's mind blocks today.

Garrett gets up at 4:00 am. As his alarm goes off, he sleepily heads straight for the shower. He takes his clothes with him into the restroom, as he doesn't want to waste any time once he is finished with this shower. Once Garrett has washed, he takes the towel and begins to dry off his body, completely dry so he can put on the clothes. This saves him some time before going down to see Brayden and Connor in the basement cells.

Now that Garrett's all dressed and ready for the day, he heads back to his room. There is something that he needs to grab from his dresser before going to the basement. He makes it to his dresser, opens the top drawer, and removes the small box he had placed in it, last night before bed. He had placed a puzzle piece in the box. Even to this day, he is still unsure of what the puzzle piece is for, but he keeps it on him at all times just in case it's needed. Garrett places the small box containing the puzzle piece into his front pocket, then closes his top dresser drawer. Now that he has everything he needs, Garrett makes his way to the elevators and to the basement.

Garrett arrives at the elevators, and he is lucky since once he presses the down button, the doors open, and the elevator is ready for a passenger. He makes his way into the elevator and presses the basement button. Next stop, the basement floor.

As Garrett exits the elevator into the basement, he reaches for the night vision goggles he has to wear since Mason keeps the lights off down in the basement. Garrett knows it is very early for the boys, but he also knows they have to have a plan in place for today. He knows they only have today to either break through Kayla's dreams or be prepared for what will happen if Brayden is unsuccessful.

"Hey, you two. It's time to get up. Come on! Get out of bed. It's only me, Garrett. It's time to get up. We need to discuss what we are going to go through today. Brayden, you are either going to break into Kayla's dreams, or we will have to fight our way out of here. We need to be prepared for both outcomes. Either way, you both have to get up. We don't have much time here alone. Maria and Maclaine, and even possibly Mason, could all be coming down here this morning. So get your butts up. NOW!" Garrett shouts to Connor and Brayden.

"Why are you yelling? You act like we have done something wrong when all we have done is sleep," Brayden tells Garrett, who has disturbed his sleeping time.

"No, you have not done anything wrong yet. But today, Mason is going to expect results from you. That means he expects you to make it into Kayla's mind today, and I have a feeling he is going to try again before she wakes up this morning. That also means we need to come up with a backup plan in case you are unable to complete your task at Mason's demands," Garrett tells the two of them.

"Why do you think he is going to try again this early? And what makes you think I won't be able to breach Kayla's thoughts this time? I already know about two of her mine blocks, the Kelly song, 'Broken Pieces,' and the younger version of Kelly sitting on the floor in a room filled with puzzle pieces. I'm sure that once I know what to do to get past young Kelly and the puzzle pieces, I will have made it to the part of Kayla's mind that Mason is expecting me to reach. But even when I do reach the real Kayla's mind, I've already said I was going to lie to Mason. So, to be honest, what does it matter if I don't actually reach her mind? I am going to lie to Mason anyway. I can just lie about breaking through her walls that have been placed on her mind, can't I?" Brayden questions Garrett as to why they need a backup plan.

"Brayden, the last thing any of us can do is to take Mason for a fool. I did not want to have to tell you this, but there are things Mason already knows. So if they don't happen the way they should, he will know you are lying," Garrett stresses to Brayden.

"And just how will Mason know what the outcome is going to be before it happens? Is there something you are leaving out that we should know about?" Brayden questions Garrett.

"Yes, there are quite a few things that both of you don't know, and I am about to reveal them now. I just need you both to trust me when I tell you that what happens from now on, Mason will know if it is the truth or not. Don't question how I know this, but believe it. Now, do we want to talk about a backup plan so we can get out of this alive if you don't succeed?" Garrett insists to Connor and Brayden.

***

It's not too long of a wait for Maria and Maclaine before the elevator reaches their floor. The elevator doors open as if it is calling them to step inside. Since the elevator is calling for them, Maria and Maclaine please it by stepping aboard. Once the pair is securely inside, Maria presses the button for the basement.

As the door begins to close, Maclaine thinks about Garrett and his whereabouts. "So, where do you think Garrett is right now?"

"I don't know, but he better be here when Mason arrives. Mason is not one to wait. If he asks for something to be done, he means business. Defying his orders is only asking for trouble," Maria clarifies to Maclaine.

Just as Maria is finishing her sentence, the elevator stops at the basement level. The doors open, allowing Maria and Maclaine to both be surprised as to what they find in the basement waiting on them.

"And just what are you doing down here already, Garrett?" Maclaine snaps at him. "Why didn't you just tell me you were already down here when I called you earlier?"

"He has been down here trying to come up with a backup plan, haven't you, Garrett?" Maria speaks before Garrett can.

"Yes, I have been down here with Connor and Brayden coming up with a plan. But how do you know that is what I was doing here? Who's to say that I'm not down here trying to tell them both a way to escape?" Garrett replies to Maria's comment.

"Because, if you were here discussing an exit strategy, the three of you would be gone already. But since you are all still here, I can assume you were coming up with a plan for the day. Am I even close, Garrett?" Maria asks with quick wit.

"You are correct, Maria. I came down earlier to ensure we have a backup plan if Brayden is unable to reach into Kayla's dreams. I also figured that Mason is going to want to try again before she wakes up this morning, which I must have been right because here you are," Garrett explains his actions to Maria and Maclaine.

"That is exactly what we were thinking. The only reason he would have us all up at this hour, and not Kayla, would have to be because he wants to try again. It's like he's being pressured by someone, but we just don't know who it could be. Mason is the leader of his people, so him answering to someone else is out of the question," Maria ends her thoughts aloud.

"I can see where you get that idea. I was thinking the same thing about Mason. But we don't have time to waste debating on if he is being bullied into something or not. That is why, at least, we have already come up with a plan if things don't go the way Mason is expecting. So, are we supposed to wait here until Mason calls for us, or should we go ahead and go up to the room next to Kayla's? This way, we can have the upper hand by already being set in position when he arrives. That will throw Mason off his game just a bit, which is something we could use today," Garrett expresses to Maria.

"I'm sure you will be filling us in on the plan you have come up with, so I won't press the issue for now. I like the thought of being in the room when Mason arrives. I believe you are correct in assuming it will shake up his authority as well as his thoughts this morning," Maria concurs with Garrett.

"What if we can try and have me connect with Kayla's dreams before Mason arrives? Maybe the defense walls are because of Mason and not because of me?" Brayden suggests to the team.

"I think that would be a great idea, Brayden," Connor speaks up.

"Then what would we tell Mason if he was to walk in, and we are already connecting with Kayla without him? What excuse can we come up with if that happens?" Maclaine questions.

"Why don't we at least go up to the room and see if we can beat Mason there before we start worrying about how to deal with him if we do something without him," Brayden again makes the suggestion.

"Sounds like a solid plan to me. Let's get a move on," Maria instructs the team.

***

Mason has waited long enough for everyone to make their way down to the basement cells where Brayden and Connor are still being held. He decides it's time to make his presence known amongst them all. Mason makes his way over to his office door, then exits, making his way down to the elevators.

Upon arrival at the elevators, Mason presses the down button. While waiting for his elevator to arrive, he cannot help but think how so many people were involved in the creation of the elevator. Otis is the only one who is given credit for its inception. Mason thinks of Alexander Miles, an African-American inventor, who was awarded a U.S. Patent on October 11, 1887, for an improved way to open and close the doors to the shaft and elevator. He hates that so many good people get overlooked throughout history because of one reason or another. He knows that Otis is not the only creator of the elevator, and by remembering the others, helps him believe in his cause even more.

About that time, his elevator arrives. Once the doors open for Mason, he steps inside and presses the button for the basement. Mason takes his slow ride as the elevator descends. He is ready to fill the group in on what is going to happen today. The elevator makes its stop on Mason's requested floor, the basement level. The doors open, letting out the light which is filling the small elevator. Since Mason has instructed everyone to meet him here, in the completely dark basement, he half expected to hear some sort of complaint about the light, since the group should already be in their night vision goggles, thus causing them blindness. To his surprise, Mason hears no complaints or anything at all down in the cell room.

"Hello? Is anyone down here?" Mason is asking out loud to the group he suspects should be down here waiting for him. *Where in the world could they have gone? They knew this is where we are supposed to meet,* Mason thinks to himself as he turns back towards the elevators to make his way back up to the main floor, the floor where his office and Kayla's room are. That also includes the room next to Kayla's. Mason is unsure but has a feeling that they may have already gone to the room without him. As the elevator stops, Mason is unexpectedly greeted by Maria.

"There you are. We have been wondering where you were, not that it's any of our business where you are. We went ahead and went into the room. We thought we would wait for you there since you didn't come to the basement cells. We figured, being this early, maybe we could make sure everyone was comfortable, especially Brayden. This way, he is more relaxed and ready for the defensive borders placed on Kayla's mind. We thought that maybe it was the stress or pressure she felt that sent the walls up in the first place. We thought that maybe if Brayden was not stressed or pressured, then Kayla may not feel it either, or let him in easier, without all the mind barriers," Maria explains to Masons.

"There sure is a lot of 'we' in your story, Maria. Is there a reason you have lost control of the group? Because to me, it sounds as if you have lost your grip on your team. Am I correct?" Mason interjects to Maria.

"No, I have not lost control over the group. They willfully do what I tell them to do. I was merely telling you what we all discussed as a team to make sure today is the best day possible for you. We don't want anything to interfere with what we do today, so we discussed today as a group would. I needed to hear all sides of what we were doing right and what we may have been doing wrong. I believe that would have been what you would have done, would you not?" Maria asks Mason while actually stalling for the others to have more time to finish what they have already accomplished.

"You are correct, Maria. I would have done the exact same thing, so good thinking. And were you able to find out anything we did not know already?" Mason questions Maria.

"Actually, yes, but I think it would be better if you see it in person, instead of me trying to explain it to you."

"Then how about you go ahead and lead me in there, so I can see for myself."

"Right this way," Maria says to Mason. She leads the way to the room, hoping the others are finished so when they walk in, Mason will see them waiting on him and not already connected with Kayla.

The two of them make their way down the hallway and to the room adjacent to Kayla's. As they arrive, Maria does not know what she will find, but turns the doorknob and slowly pushes the door open. Maria and Mason are stunned as to what they are seeing.

Chapter 4

Playing Dead?

Ian, Kenzie, and Jax left the Sky Lounge and made their way down to Jax's quarters since they are the largest. The three of them have been trying to come up with the perfect questions to ask Garrett when they have him back into Ian's body, which will be soon.

"I think I need to talk to Junior again before Garrett takes over my body," Ian relays to Kenzie and Jax.

"And why would you need to do that? I don't think there is much Junior can do for us. The last time we tried to contact him, we ended up seeing him for the first time, twice. Then we ended up forty-five minutes in the past. There is no telling what could happen if you try to contact Junior again," Kenzie spouts out in fear.

"When Garrett was here for the first time, he said someone was in my head trying to stop him from gaining access to my body. That leaves it open for too many questions about Junior, especially with what Garrett can do. I need to tell Junior to stay in the shadows and let Garrett do what he needs to while he is in my body. Also, I can see if there is a way for Junior to be able to force Garrett to answer our questions, truthfully, without being caught or causing any undue damage," Ian makes a very bold suggestion and a risky one at that.

"That has to be one of the best ideas you have ever had, Ian. That is a risk worth taking, but you better do it now!" Jax exclaims with excitement.

"Okay, now just let me go in and talk to Junior and jump right back out. Is that okay with the two of you?" Ian asks.

Jax and Kenzie can only nod their heads with a, yes, and that is all Ian needs to continue.

Ian takes a swift move over to Jax's bed and climbs up onto it. Secretly Ian is wishing Jax would have bought that new bed setting at Bed, Bath & Beyond, but this will have to do. Ian gets comfortable on Jax's bed and closes his eyes. He begins to think of Kayla, then Junior. Ian knows he is pressed for time, but that will not mean anything to Junior. So, Ian tries to relax to just dream. That is when it happens. That's when Junior makes himself present.

"Ian, what in the world are you doing skydiving? You have never been skydiving before. I'm here, so what is it that you need from me?" Junior asks Ian as they are both free-falling through the sky.

Just before Ian can answer Junior's question, they are not skydiving anymore but standing together in a regular room, maybe a library. "I need you to do me a favor. In a few minutes, someone is going to take over my mind and body. I need you to let him take over. I need you to stay in the shadows of my mind, and, if you can without being caught, make this person answer our questions this time," Ian asks of Junior.

"I'm not sure if I understand everything that you are asking, but I can do my best," Junior reassures Ian.

"That's all I can ask of you, Junior. Just don't put yourself in harm's way. Now, you should go and hide somewhere in my mind and wait for him to arrive," Ian tells Junior.

"How do you know that this person is going to be coming for sure?" Junior asks Ian before leaving for his hiding spot.

"Because he has already done it once before," Ian says to Junior in a playful tone. Then Ian wakes up. "Okay, Junior is as ready as he is going to be with what little time I had to fill him in on everything that is going on, which is not much."

"So now we just wait for Garrett to show up?" Kenzie questions.

"Yes, but it shouldn't be much longer now. I promise," Ian comforts Kenzie.

***

"I think we should go ahead and get into the same position we were in the first time and start talking about the way we got here," Ian says to Jax and Kenzie.

"But this is not where he brought us, remember? He brought us back to Brayden and your room. What do you think he will say if he gets here and we are not in the same room?" Kenzie brings up.

"Kenzie, you are right. We need to hurry down to my room, and NOW!" Ian shouts at the others. "We need to go now because we do not have much time left," Ian tells the other two, as he has made his way over Jax's bedroom door, opening the door as he completes his sentence.

Jax and Kenzie take Ian's, not so subtle, cues and make their way to the door as well. Once the three of them are out of Jax's room, Ian closes the door, and they make their way quickly over to the elevators. They know they need to go up to Brayden and Ian's room. They don't have enough time to take the stairs, so the elevator is their only option. Upon arrival at the elevators, Ian has already pressed the up button, so now they wait.

It was not long before the elevator reached their floor. Once it did and the doors opened, the three of them jumped inside, and Ian pressed the button to his floor. The door closes, and they begin their ascend to Ian's floor, with the hope of not having to stop for anyone else going up today. They are in luck as they keep the elevator to themselves. It does not stop on any other floor, except for Ian and Brayden's floor. As the elevator stops and the doors open, they all rush out and walk quickly, straight to Ian's room.

"Hurry up and open the door, Ian. You know we don't have much time left to get into place," Kenzie demands of Ian at his bedroom door.

"I'm trying. Give me a second to put the key in the door, will, ya, Kenzie," Ian snaps back. Just then, the key slips into the door keyhole and Ian is able to open it. As soon as the door is open, the three of them try to enter the room, all at the same time, and wind up stuck in the doorframe.

"We need to enter one at a time, or we will never get in," Ian suggests.

With Ian's suggestion, they all back out of the doorframe. First, Kenzie enters, then Jax, followed by Ian, so he can pull the bedroom door shut and lock it at the same time. They only have a few minutes to get into place, so they all take a seat in the room where they were the first time they met Garrett.

Once in place, Jax tells them to start talking. That's when it all starts to happen... again.

***

Looking through the open door, Mason and Maria are both standing in shock at what they are seeing. Neither of them can believe what they see. The four people Maria left in the room were all now sleeping for some reason.

Brayden was asleep on the bed, Connor asleep on a soft chair beside the bed, and Maclaine and Garrett were asleep on the floor.

"What in the world is going on here, Maria? Is this some of your doing?" Mason inquires.

"They were all awake when I left them to go get you, and that was just a few minutes ago. I have no idea what this is. None of them have this kind of power, the power to put everyone to sleep. Could someone on your team have done this, Mason?" Maria inquires right back to him.

"Absolutely not! And if they could, they would never defy me by doing such a thing. Right now, we need to find a way to wake them up. Do you have any suggestions?"

Without a word, Maria walks over to Garrett, since he is the closest to her, nudges him with her foot. "Garrett! Garrett, what are you doing sleeping right now?" Maria shouts while still prodding him with her foot, but gets no response.

"Mason, I am at a loss for words as to what is happening here," Maria confesses to Mason.

With those words, the two of them could do nothing but stand and stare at each other in disbelief.

***

Garrett instructs, "Here's the plan for now, everyone. While Maria is running interference with Mason, so we can gain some time with Brayden connecting with Kayla's mind, we are all going to pretend we are asleep until he is finished. So while you are asleep, Brayden, or actually dream-walking with Kayla, we will all be pretending to be asleep as well. Connor, you will take the big sofa chair by the bed, and of course, Brayden you will take the bed. To make it look like someone has put us to sleep, or it's unnatural, Maclaine and I will take the floor in odd places. So when they come back and find us this way, they will not know what to think or what to do. That will buy us as much time as we can get. They won't hurt us, so don't worry about that. All of you have to make sure you don't make a move in any way if they start yelling or pushing us. We have to 'play dead' in a way.

"Now, once Brayden wakes up, then we can get up, and Brayden will only get up if he is successful with connecting with Kayla, or he knows he can't. Either way, we know Brayden has done what he can, and we can wake up then. Does everyone understand the plan?" Garrett finishes.

"You got it," Brayden replies as everyone takes their place for the theatrical performance of the year.

As they are all in place and pretending to be asleep, the door to the bedroom opens.

Showtime, Garrett thinks to himself.

***

"What if they didn't get a time reset for them, and Garrett is in no position to come to us now? Then what do we do?" Kenzie asks out loud.

"Don't think that way ..." Ian stops mid-sentence.

"What am I doing here again?" Garrett asks with Ian's voice and body.

"What are you talking about, Ian? That is exactly what I am trying to find out. Now, how did you and Kenzie escape from Maria's room?" Jax is now acting as if this is the first time meeting Garrett.

"You already know how they got here, Jax! I have already explained it to you all not long ago," Garrett tells Jax.

"Ian, you have not explained anything yet, nor has Kenzie. You both claim you can't remember how you got here. Or that is what you both keep telling me, and I don't believe either of you. There has to be more to the story that you are both leaving out," Jax plays the game with this reply.

"Stop calling me Ian if you don't mind," Garrett says to Jax.

"Then what would you like to be called?" Now Jax is getting somewhere.

"Call me by my name, Garrett. You already know who I am, so why am I here and why do you not remember the first time I was here? It was about an hour ago. I explained how I have been helping you all along. I was in the middle of a mission and was pulled to Ian and Kenzie's sleeping bodies because Kenzie showed up where I was while I was in Kayla's body trying to steal something from Mason's safe. So I used Ian's body to carry Kenzie's here to get them out of harm's way. You really don't remember any of this?" Garrett asks.

There are some things I do remember, but there is one thing you just said that you would not answer the first time, Ian thinks to Garrett.

"And just what was that Ian?"

That you were in Kayla's body during your mission, and now we know why Kenzie was drawn to you and that body at that time, Ian thinks to Garrett, who is using his body right now.

"So, this is a trick? You know that I have been here before, and yet you risk another mission of mine for your own reasons? I can't stay here. I have to get back to my current mission right now. Do you understand?" Garrett is fuming with anger.

"Yes, we know you have been here before, actually, at this exact moment in time. We can't explain it, but Ian, Kenzie, and I are forty-five minutes behind everyone else in the timeline again. You are here not because of us, but because you came here at this time on your own. The same time you came here for the first time," Jax tells Garrett. "So, no, this is not a trick. We are just more prepared for your arrival this time."

"I don't understand what you are talking about. How can you three be forty-five minutes behind everyone else? That does not even seem possible," Garrett says.

"Says the guy from the future," Kenzie says to Garrett before anyone else could speak.

"The future? What are you getting to there, Kenzie?" Jax asks before Garrett could even say a word in defense.

"Garrett will tell you in just a second. The only way he could have helped you and Ian on the train, and know as much as he does, but can't share any of his information, is because he is from the future. Am I right, Garrett?" Kenzie asks with confidence.

"I don't know how you have been able to come up with such an outlandish conclusion, but it is absurd. There is no way I am from the future. I just have gifts like the rest of you. There is nothing special about me," Garrett tries to convey to the three of them.

"The way you helped Ian and me on the train, to hide in plain sight from Mason's goons, your timing was too perfect to just show up when you did and have us sit down just so quickly. The only conclusion that can be determined from those actions alone would be that you already knew what was going to happen because you are from the future. So Kenzie's assessments of you are not that far off," Jax lays all his cards on the table.

"Okay, if you want to know about me, then how about you tell me about Junior? Who is he, and where did he come from, and how is he involved in any of this?" Garrett is asking out loud, but the questions are really directed to Ian. "How about it, Ian? Care to exchange information?"

What makes you think that I or any of the others know anything about someone named Junior? Ian thinks back to Garrett.

"Yeah, what makes you think we know someone named Junior?" Kenzie shouts out at what Ian is thinking.

"How do you know what Ian and I are talking about, Kenzie?" Garrett asks.

"Because I was listening to Ian's thoughts while you were so quiet. I figured you were talking to Ian, and since not all of us can hear thoughts, I decided to step in and listen. It seems like I did the right thing," Kenzie explains to Garrett.

"Well, then out with the truth, or I will say no more. And I know you all know who Junior is. But if you don't admit to knowing him, you will get no more information from me. By the way, I can feel Junior lurking somewhere in your mind, Ian. If you want to know how I know that, then answer me honestly."

Fine, you win. I don't want to reveal too much about Junior because we almost lost him once in our timeline. Let's say he is from our future, and we want to make sure he stays that way. He was helping us well before Kayla was erased from history, Ian thinks to Garrett and Kenzie, who has patched Jax in for this conversation.

"Okay, I'll give you that, about not wanting to reveal too much about Junior. I can feel that his life does depend on if we all succeed or fail. So, yes, I am from 'a' future. It's not like anything you know or need to think about. My future is different from yours. Do you understand?" Garrett clarifies out loud to the group.

"I have no clue what type of future you are talking about if it's not like ours," Jax says to Garrett.

"We all have a future, but I am not from your present, so therefore I am not from your future. You are going to have to leave it at that," Garrett tells Jax.

"Yes, we will leave it at that," Jax replies.

"Yes, I am from 'a' future. To my world, you are a history assignment. I have been assigned to this time period and people. I am a student from my school sent here as part of my history assignment to study history. But I fear a bully in my school has come back as well and is trying to upset the balance of time and make me fail by changing the past. That is forbidden in my world. In my world, we already know how this history begins and ends, but if it is changed in any way, then my final report will be worthless. Do any of you understand what I am talking about?" Garrett asks the group.

"I'm not going to say we do, or don't, fully understand, but we will respect what you ask now. Sorry we gave you so much trouble earlier," Kenzie tells Garrett.

"No problem, now that you retrieved all the information you were looking for, I am going to have to go back to my new mission, or what I like to call my current mission. So if you don't mind, it was a pleasure meeting you all again for the first time, the second time," Garrett says to Kenzie, Jax, and Ian, just before he leaves Ian's body.

"Ian? Has he left?" Jax asks.

"Yes, Garrett is gone. He has left my body. Do you two think that was what we were supposed to ask Garrett? You know, about our extra forty-five minutes?" Ian asks Jax and Kenzie.

As Kenzie is looking down at the watch on her wrist, she turns her attention back to Ian and says, "I will take a wild guess and say yes. I am pretty sure we did exactly what we were supposed to do," Kenzie finishes.

"And just how do you know for a fact that we have completed what we were supposed to do?" Jax asks Kenzie.

"Look at your watches. Notice anything different about the time?"

"The time has moved up forty-five minutes. We are now back up with the current timeline!" Ian shouts. "The only thing left for us to figure out is how that helps us. It must help us in some way or another, or we would not have been given the extra time to speak to Garrett again, then have time reset for us once we did."

"Unless time was always going to reset, regardless of if we asked the right questions or not. Did you think of that? Maybe we were given this one shot, and win or lose, time was going to reset. We all just need to sit down and discuss his answers and see how they can help us now," Jax tells Ian, with a mood killer.

"Way to keep a positive look on things, Jax!" Kenzie shouts. "Ian don't listen to Jax right now. Let's all go back down to his room, so we can have a lot more space, and put all of our thoughts together, including Junior's," Kenzie suggests.

Chapter 5

Brian?

"What do we do now? Where should we start first?" Kenzie asks, now that they are back down in Jax's slightly larger room. "Do we want to contact Junior and see what he knows about Garrett, or do we want to sit and talk about the answers Garrett gave this time, which is what Ian is about to suggest."

"Let me make a phone call really quick, and then we can see where to go from there," Jax says to Ian and Kenzie.

The two of them give Jax a look of complete confusion about how he could call for someone to help them in a situation like this. But they both slowly give a head nod for yes to answer Jax's question.

Jax picks up his room phone, dials only a few numbers, and listens to the ringing. Jax listens until the voice on the other end says, "Hello, this is Brian. How can I help you today?"

"Hello, Brian, it's me, Jax. I am here with two students, and we could really use your help right now. Are you busy?"

"Not at the moment. You have actually caught me on one of my lighter days between work and charity. Do you want to come down to my office, or do I need to make a house call?"

"If it's no trouble for you, do you mind coming up to my room? As I mentioned before, I am with two students, and we all could use your help."

"I am on my way, Jax. Please make sure none of you do anything until I get there. Do you understand me?" Brian says as he hangs up his end of the phone, not waiting for an answer. He then begins to make a run to his office door. Brian is so worried about Jax and the two students, he does not even remember if he shut his office door. He is making a mad dash to the elevator because he knows time is of the essence.

"Okay, I have a friend coming up here right now that I believe can help us figure out what we need to do next. He is a counselor that started here at the school about three years ago. Since he has begun his career here with us, he has helped more students and teachers through some of their toughest decisions and choices of their lives. Every one of them said without his words of wisdom, they never would have known what to do. His name is Brian, and he has asked that we do nothing until he arrives. I agree with him. Do you both think we can do nothing until he arrives?" Jax explains who Brian is to Kenzie and Ian and his instructions.

Kenzie and Ian both agree with Jax, or more like with Brian's advice, for now, to do nothing, and decide to wait for him. They are both intrigued by what it is that Brian can do. But before the two of them can talk telepathically to each other, there is a knock at the door.

Jax heads to his bedroom door as quickly as he can so he can unlock it and open it for who he hopes is Brian. As the lock turns and Jax opens his door, he is relieved to see Brian standing there. Brian has dark hair and dark eyes, a strong jawline, covered with a short line of dark facial hair all around the side and bottom of his chin. With his stocky build, infectious smile, and rosy cheeks, anyone could tell why Brian was once one of Jax's favorite former students.

"Well, aren't you going to invite me in?" Brian asks Jax, who is just staring at him at the door.

"Yes, I'm sorry to make you stand out in the hall like that when I'm the one that called you up here. Please come in," Jax apologizes to Brian while ushering him into his sleeping quarters. "Please take a seat, anywhere you like."

"Thank you, Jax, and just who might you two be?" Brian asks the two students he does not have the privilege of knowing while he takes a seat at Jax's eating table.

For a second, Kenzie and Ian were not sure who Brian was speaking to because they both felt like they had known him for years. So they both look around the room to see if anyone else is in there with them, but they come up empty. Brian is speaking to them as they realized. "Oh, you are asking us who WE are. Well, I am Ian, and this is Kenzie."

"Well, it's very nice to meet you both. I hope I can be of some assistance today for all of you. I'm not sure what Jax has had time to tell you about me, but I'm the school counselor. What I do is listen and help people figure out which decision is the best for them. Now I don't make the choices for them or suggest one or another. I honestly just listen and ask them six words, "What do you have to lose?" I can't tell you any more than that, but it's an amazing process that helps them decide on their own," Brian finishes.

"It's nice to meet you as well, Brian. Are you sure we have not met before? I feel like we have," Kenzie is the first to speak after Brian has finished.

"I can assure you that this is the first time I have ever met either of you. But it's okay because I get that all the time. So, what is it that I can help you three with today?"

"Well, we have a dilemma. We are short on time, but we have a couple of options, we don't know which one is the best. We don't have time for all three. We need your guidance on which direction we should go that will give us the biggest advantage for what we need to do next," Jax expresses to Brian.

"That's a tall order. Where should we start? Do you want to start with where Ian wants to talk about the answers Garrett gave this time? Or how about we start with Kenzie's idea and go straight to Junior to see what he knows about Garrett? Even better, we can do what Jax has not told either of you, but to just wait and see what happens, to see what time presents to you on its own terms?" Brian reveals all of the team's motives to each other.

"And how do you know all of these things about each of us? We have not even had the chance to tell you what our dilemma is, but yet you just told each of us what we already know. The only problem is that you have not been here for any of what you just said, and you did not get any of that from Jax on the phone. So how do you know these things about us?" Ian asks Brian with a hint of fear.

"It's a gift I have. I can feel what people truly want deep in their hearts, even if they don't know it at the time. I did not mean to offend anyone, but I was just speaking what I was feeling from each of you," Brian explains to the group.

"Sorry, Brian, I have not had a chance to tell them about exactly what it is that you can do. We are in such a rush that it never crossed my mind. But now that you know that we all want to explore different avenues, what do you suggest will be the best way for us to proceed?" Jax asks Brian.

"That is a hard question to answer because all of you have very compelling reasons to choose the path that you want. I must say that all of your reasons are very hard for someone to choose one. Remember the process I mentioned earlier? The one about "What do you have to lose?" Well, this exercise will be perfect for all of you to figure out what you need to do. You will all come to the same conclusion by the end of it. It's not a magic trick because deep down in all of your minds, you all know what the true answer is already. I am merely going to help you find that answer in your mind. Do you all understand, and do I have your permission to perform this process with each of you?" Brian asks of the group.

"I'm sure we are all fine with this, as long as it doesn't take too long because we do not have much time," Ian answers Brian for all of them.

"It will take less time than the three of you following your own paths for answers, or you keep debating on what to do between the three of your suggestions. So how does that sound? Especially for people who are short on time. I'm offering you the quickest way to resolve your dilemma. So now that we have resolved the time issue, who wants to go first?" Brian asks a quiet room, as they are all three hanging on to his every word.

"Okay, now that I have all of your attention, who would like to start?" Brian asks the mesmerized trio staring at him again.

"I will go first if that is okay with the others," Kenzie is the first to speak up.

Both Jax and Ian just look at each other and then nod to agree with Kenzie's request.

With their look of approval, Kenzie stands up from her seat and walks over to Brian with no fear. She can feel deep down inside herself that Brian is not there to hurt them but to honestly help them in any way he can. That feeling within her comforts her upon her approach to Brian. As Kenzie approaches him, Brian begins to move into position, standing in the center of the rug. Brian holds his arms out while instructing Kenzie to stand directly in front of him.

Now that Brian and Kenzie are in place for the exercise, he begins.

"Alright, Kenzie, are you okay?"

"Yes, I am very relaxed and fine."

"Now, I am just going to ask you the same set of questions, over and over again, no matter what answer you give me. Once you get down to the heart of the answer within yourself, the one you already know, then don't answer my question again.

Do you understand? Just say thank you, and you may go and sit back down. Don't reveal your answer to anyone, as we will do it as a group after everyone has come to their own conclusion. I'm confident that all your answers will be the same, but we will see. Now, are you ready to begin?"

"Yes, I am ready to begin."

"Okay, Kenzie, what is it that you think you all should do now?"

"I think we need to talk to Junior."

"Now, what do you have to lose by talking to Junior first?"

"What?"

"Think about what you could lose by talking to Junior first."

"I could lose more time if Junior does not know anymore more than we already do."

"What do you have to lose by losing more time?"

"I could end up wasting what little time we already have by talking to someone, who if he did know anything, would have already told us. Just like he always has in the past."

"And what do you have to lose by wasting what little time you have on something you will find out from Junior, in due time, if he knows anything anyway?"

"Thank you, Brian. I understand now," Kenzie expresses gratitude as she walks back over to her spot on the couch and takes her seat.

Before Brian can ask who will be next, Ian pops up right in front of him. "I take it that you are ready?"

"Yes, I am ready."

"Did you hear the instructions I gave to Kenzie? Because they are going to apply to you as well."

"Yes, I heard, and I understand the instructions of this exercise."

"Then let's get started. So, Ian, what is it that you believe you all should do with the little time you have left?"

"I think we should go over the new answers and compare them with Garrett's previous answers, to see if we can learn where they are," Ian says with confidence that his idea will be the choice they all agree on in the end.

"And what do you have to lose if you don't compare Garrett's answers?"

"Well, I'm sure we will find out much-needed information."

"That is not what I asked, now is it? I asked, what do you have to lose by not comparing Garrett's answers?"

"Fine, I would lose time if Garrett's answers do not get us any closer to where we are now to finding our friends."

"And what do you have to lose by losing time on Garrett's answers not getting you anywhere closer to your friends?"

"Well, the longer we are from them, the more harm that could come to them."

"And what do you have to lose by possibly being the cause of them being harmed?"

"Thank you, Brian, for helping me understand that no matter how much I want my suggestion to be the one we go with, but it's clear now I was wrong to try to force it. You are

AMAZING!" Ian exclaims to Brian as he is walking off to take his seat on the couch.

As Jax has not gotten up from his seat, Brian has to ask, "Are you ready for your turn, Jax?"

"It's okay, Brian. I have already done the exercise twice, and both times I have come to the same conclusion, which is not the one with which I started. I'm pretty sure that I have come to the same conclusion as Ian and Kenzie. I hope that is okay with you," Jax explains to Brian.

"It never really matters how you come to the correct answer, as long as you come to it. Sometimes people need a little help to see the difference between what they think they want, what they truly want, and what they are actually searching for," Brian says to all three of them. "I'm sure you all have some things to discuss, so if you don't need me anymore this evening, I'm going to head back down to my office. I'm sure I have a line of students waiting for me. Now you know if you need me for anything else, all you have to do is call, and I will be up here in a snap," Brian says to Jax, Kenzie, and Ian as he walks out of the bedroom door, closing it behind him as he leaves.

"So, I guess we all have the same idea now?" Jax asks Ian and Kenzie.

"If you are talking about using Maria's room to set a trap for her, so we can get some real information, then yes, we are all thinking about the same thing," Ian spits out.

"Oh, my, gosh, Ian, that is exactly what I came up with during Brian's exercise. How is that even possible?" Kenzie asks Ian.

"I don't know how he did that, but he did. Jax, what about you? Are we correct with our conclusions about Maria's room? Is it the same thought for you?" Ian asks Jax.

"I have to say, yes. That is what I came up with, not only once, but twice. During both of your exercises with Brian, I was doing the same thing in my head. And both times came up with that exact same conclusion. That is why I called Brian up here in the first place. I knew he would be able to help all of us come to the same idea. Now that we all know what we need to do, how are we going to set this trap for Maria?" Jax asks.

"Well, we know her room is all set up with alarms and defenses for anyone who tries to enter her room. Since we know these things, we can now use them to our advantage. With that being said, we now must figure out how we are going to set off Maria's defenses and alarms," Ian finishes.

"What do you mean, Ian? We have done it before, so why can't we do it again?" Kenzie asks.

"You remember what happened to both of us the last time we entered Maria's room? We were both knocked out, and Garrett had to come to take over my body and have me carry you out of her room and back into my room. Any of that ring a bell?"

"You don't have to be such a jerk about it, Ian. Of course, I remember what Garrett told us. But what if we go in while holding our breath and leave after we think enough time has passed to set off her alarms? We could even lay on the floor and pretend to be knocked out, while Jax is holding the door cracked open the entire time," Kenzie finishes explaining her plan of action. "It's either that or we get someone to actually go into Maria's room, let them pass out while we all wait nearby to grab Maria when she gets there to check things out. Which do you think would be better?"

"I have to say, I agree with Kenzie's idea much more than involving an innocent person in our troubles. Don't you think so, Ian?" Jax asks.

"Yes, Kenzie's way sounds much safer and easier for us to control. But I have just a little bit more we can add to Kenzie's plan to make it just a little more real. Trust me, it's nothing major, but simple is usually the best-laid plan," Ian answers.

"Then let's get to work. We don't have much time," Jax instructs the others as he is ready to prepare for Maria's arrival.

Chapter 6

S.C.U.B.A?

"So, what are we supposed to do while they are asleep?" Mason asks Maria.

"I guess we just wait. We wait until at least one of them wakes up," Maria replies to Mason.

"And how long do we have to wait for one of them to wake up? A few minutes, hours, days, or weeks even? Do you have any clue at all how long we may have to wait?" Mason asks Maria.

"I guess we'll just have to wait to find out, won't we?" Maria replies.

***

"Hello? Is anyone here? Kayla, can you hear me? It's me, Brayden. You may not know me, but we know someone in common. His name is Ian. Does his name ring a bell with you?" Brayden asks Kayla's figure that has materialized in the corner of her mind.

"Yes, I remember you. You were here twice. Once when Kelly was singing 'Broken Pieces,' and the second time was when you came in and found Kelly sitting on the floor full of pieces of puzzles," Kayla answers back.

"How do you know about that moment?" Brayden asks.

"Well, we are in my mind, so it would make sense if it became a memory for me, wouldn't you say? And because I was hiding behind a false wall when Kelly was sitting on the floor with the puzzle pieces," Kayla explains with laughter.

"Why didn't you say you were there? Why did you have to make it into a big joke? I am here to try and not only help you now but also save Connor and myself. Do you still feel this is a fun game?" Brayden expresses the importance to Kayla.

"I'm sorry, Brayden. I was there when they brought the two of you into this dreadful place. I was also supposed to go down to the basement cells with Mason to help interrogate you both. But I came up with an excuse as to why I could not go at that very moment, so Mason went alone, I believe. I hope they have not hurt either of you. From what I could gather, after being erased from history, was that I was supposed to be the only person to help Mason get to Ian. No one ever mentioned innocent people, like you and Connor, being involved or hurt. I hope you can believe me," Kayla explains to Brayden.

"Yes, I believe you, Kayla. We all do. That is why I am here talking to you before Mason makes me. What I need from you is to allow me in, just me, and whatever questions I ask you if it is something you don't want Mason to know, lie to me, and make it a lie that I would not be able to tell is a lie. It should be easy, because I don't know anything about you, not really anyway. Once I have all his answers and I wake up, he will interrogate me, very formidably to make sure I am telling him the truth of what you tell me. So, if you tell me a lie, and I don't know it's a lie, then I can tell Mason as if it is the truth. But if you tell a lie and I can tell, then I will have to lie to Mason. Now, I am good at telling a lie, but Mason somehow can tell when someone is telling a lie, even though I'm confident I can get a few lies past him. So do you think you can lie, lie like you are telling the truth?" Brayden asks Kayla.

"I'm a teenage girl. I've been lying to my parents for years, or at least I used to when I still had parents. So to answer your question, yes, I can lie just fine to you."

"Good, now one other thing. When I first come back, I need you to be dreaming. You see, I am a dream-walker. Mason knows this and may actually ask what you were dreaming about when I entered your sleep, so make sure it's of nothing to do with anything against Mason. Also, make sure that your dreams are not of any of us that are trying to help you now. Try to think of things from here and of Mason, and that's it. Got it?"

"Okay, I understand. How long do we have before all of this is supposed to go down? I want to make use of the time I have to prepare," Kayla asks Brayden.

"Not very long, I suspect. I'm sure once I wake up and the others do as well, Mason will only question us for a minute or so, then he will want me to dream-walk you on his behalf, so start getting ready now. Consider this your advanced notice, because now I have to leave for the time being. But you know I won't be gone very long, then I will be back again. This time to ask real questions, like we discussed," Brayden finishes up explaining to Kayla before leaving her behind and waking up on the bed.

"What happened? One minute we were all getting here, Maria went to get Mason, and that's the last thing I remember," Brayden says out loud, which is his cue for the others to know he is awake now, and they can get up as well.

"Yes, what exactly did happen? Why were all of you sleeping when you should have been preparing for what we need to do today?" Mason asks the group with disappointment in his tone.

"I was going to ask you that, Maria. Was there something you did to ensure that we all stayed here while you went off to retrieve Mason?" Maclaine questions Maria.

"I can assure you all that I had nothing to do with this. Now, we can stand around for the rest of the day asking the same question and getting the same answer, but I think we need to focus on what we are here to do. Since you are finished with your naps," Maria replies to everyone to get her point across.

"Maria is correct. We have wasted enough time already, between your naps and trying to figure out why you went to sleep in the first place. Brayden, since you are already in position, why don't you lie back and try to connect with Kayla?" Mason decides to take control of the group again.

Without another word, Brayden takes his place on the bed and closes his eyes. Brayden knows he can make contact with Kayla since he already has, but he has to put on a show for Mason. Brayden needs to make it seem real, just like the last time, and break through Kayla's mind blocks.

While everyone else is sitting or standing around Brayden, he begins to toss and turn and mumble words. The words he is saying are hard to understand, but everyone can understand 'Kelly.' The next thing he starts mumbling is about a puzzle piece. Brayden is putting on quite a show for Mason. He is now just hoping that Mason is buying his performance.

"Kayla? Are you here?" Brayden asks with his mind so only Kayla can hear him.

"Yes, I'm right here. How did it go, you know, once you woke up? Did Mason buy it?" Kayla asks back.

"So far, so good. I don't think he suspects anything. He has not told me exactly what he wants me to get from you. Mason has only told me to try and make a connection with you. I figure after making this connection, I should wake up and let Mason know I've made the connection and see what his instructions are. What do you think?" Brayden asks Kayla.

"I agree with you. Mason has to have some agenda for you to walk my dreams. If you have not been told what his plan is yet, then you are correct. Mason is first trying to access my mind. Why don't you go ahead and leave me and go back to Mason and the others? Let Mason know you now have access to my mind, and then ask him what he wants you to do next," Kayla suggests to Brayden.

"Are you sure you are ready for this, Kayla? Remember, you need to lie to me if it's something Mason asks me to find out from you since we don't want him to know the truth. I cannot know that you are lying. That's how good you have to be. I'm sure he will not ask me anything about you that I know to be true, because unlike Ian, I actually don't know you. Your lies have to be the truth to me because Mason will interrogate me once this is all done. But I won't have to lie if I tell Mason the truth, even if it's a fake truth, because I won't know the difference. Do you understand?" Brayden confirms with Kayla.

"Yes, I understand. You know that you are a very smart person," Kayla replies.

"Thank you, Kayla. I appreciate that," Brayden says back to Kayla.

Kayla just starts laughing. Then she says, "See, you already believe my lies!"

"Very funny, Kayla. I'm going to go ahead and wake up so I can find out what my next assignment is from Mason. I will see you again soon," Brayden tells Kayla. He was not too happy about the joke she just played on him.

Brayden woke up with the room full of onlookers who had been watching him make contact with Kayla. "Hello, everyone. Can someone figure out this riddle: 'The man who follows the crowd will usually get no further than the crowd, but the man who walks alone will find himself in places no one has ever imagined.'?" Brayden asks the group just for some fun. He wants to make it look like he had to pass these tests in order to enter the final block in Kayla's mind. "Or how about this one: 'From where you're standing, how far IS where you'd like to be?'"

"What in the world are you talking about? Why are you asking about these simple sayings? What do they have to do with you trying to connect with Kayla's mind?" Mason is answering Brayden's questions with questions of his own.

"These were the tests I had to pass to make a connection with Kayla. And yes, I made a connection with Kayla's dreams. I can now access her mind with no more walls blocking me or tests to pass. So now that I have access to Kayla, what would you like me to do while I am in her mind?" Brayden asks Mason.

"We will get to that in due time. Right now, I want to make sure you can go in and exit Kayla's dreams with no problems. Are you completely sure you will have no issues when you try to go back in, and when it's time for you to leave, you will be able to exit with the information I send you in there to retrieve?" Mason needs more clarification.

"Mason, why are you questioning the boy? If he says he has done it already and can do it again, that should be all the proof you need. I can assure you that his word is enough for me because he knows what's at stake if he is not telling the truth," Maria chimed in with her own opinion.

"I have to say that I agree with Maria on this. I don't believe the boy is going to lie about something as important as this. I think it's time you told him what it is that you are looking for in the mind of your special guest," Maclaine backs up Maria.

"Fine, you have all made your points very clear. We will proceed with the plan. I will go ahead and give Brayden his exact assignment if that is okay..." Mason is cut off by Maria.

"Mason, can you wait just a little bit longer?" Maria asks.

"First you want me to hurry up, now you want me to wait. What's going on with you, Maria?" Mason asks back to Maria.

"Let's just say I have to head back to my room at the school. My alarms have been set off, and we know who is left, don't we?" Maria tells Mason.

"In that case, yes, we can wait for a bit longer. You need to get to the school as quickly as possible to find out who you have captured now and get back here as fast as you can. Do you understand? Kayla will not sleep forever," Mason informs Maria.

"Here, let me take care of that for you," Maria says to Mason. Then Maria places her hands on the wall between the two rooms and speaks some chant the others don't understand. Once she has completed chanting, she looks over at Mason and says, "Now she will be asleep until I wake her. Are you satisfied?"

"Very, now go before you end up with an empty room again," Mason tells Maria.

Maria takes his advice and makes her exit from the room, then exits the compound to make her way to her room at the school.

***

"So, are we just going to go up to Maria's room, break-in, and hold our breath? How long can you hold your breath, Ian?" Kenzie asks.

"Well, not as long as we are going to need to be in Mara's room. Jax, what are we going to do for us to be able to stay in Maria's room long enough for us to catch her?" Ian is now asking Jax for advice.

"I have an idea, but you both have to give me about twenty minutes. Can you do that for all of us?" Jax asks Ian and Kenzie since they don't have the best record for following orders.

"Yes, Jax. We will give you however long you need. We will not do anything until you return. We have learned our lesson about not following orders," Ian tells Jax.

"All right then. I will be back as fast as I can. You two be mindful and don't do anything until I get back. Promise me," Jax pleads with Ian and Kenzie.

"We promise, Jax," Kenzie answers for the both of them.

With that promise, Jax leaves the room to destinations unknown to Ian and Kenzie. "What do we do now?" Kenzie asks Ian.

"We wait until Jax gets back and see what he gets that is going to help us on our mission. He said he would only be gone for twenty minutes, so we should at least give him that before we start to worry about anything else. Do you agree?"

"Yes, but what if he is not back in twenty minutes? Then what do we do? We don't even know where Jax went," Kenzie expresses to Ian.

"Well, right now, we just wait. We will worry about anything that happens, or doesn't happen, after twenty minutes," Ian replies to a nervous Kenzie.

Kenzie agrees with Ian and they both begin to wait for twenty minutes for Jax to return. Which, luckily for them, they do not have to wait for the entire twenty minutes before Jax returns.

"What are you carrying with you? Where exactly did you go?" Ian questions Jax about the supplies he has brought back for them.

"Let's just say I went down to the diving storage room. These are oxygen tanks that you can both wear when you enter Maria's room. You can both pretend to pass out on her room floor. But instead of trying to hold your breath, you will be able to continue breathing until Maria arrives. I will be standing at the bedroom door, holding it open, until Maria arrives. Then I will have to let the door shut and take a position in the hallway where she will not see me when she exits the elevator," Jax explains his unusual gear for this mission.

"That sounds perfect. But we were wondering how we were going to stay in Maria's room long enough for her to come back and find someone there on her floor. Now, these scuba tanks and masks will allow us to stay in there as long as the air in the tanks lasts," Ian tells Jax.

"So, does this mean we are ready to go to Maria's room and get this started?" Kenzie inquires to anyone who will answer.

"Yes, it's time to gear up and head to Maria's floor. But only if you are both ready for this and are sure you are prepared to have this encounter with Maria. Remember, I was told to help Maria when the time comes for me to do so," Jax states.

With those words being said by Jax, Ian and Kenzie begin to walk over to the bedroom door. Ian has picked up the diving gear and breathing masks. That is their way of telling Jax they are ready to get this mission started and see if Maria takes the bait.

Jax takes their subtle gestures and gets a move on behind Ian and Kenzie to the bedroom door. He is just as ready as they are.

Now that they are all in the hallway, they proceed to the elevators. They know they need to go down to Maria's floor, so once they arrive at the elevators, Ian presses the down button, and they wait.

Once the elevator stops on their floor, they all enter it. They are happy that the elevator is empty. So Jax presses the button for Maria's floor, and they wait for their ride down. Their ride is quick because the elevator makes no other stops.

Upon arrival on Maria's floor, as the elevator doors open, they all exit and make their way to Maria's room. Once they arrive at Maria's room, Jax goes ahead and takes care of the lock on the door. Now that the door is open, Kenzie and Ian make their way in while wearing their scuba gear Jax acquired from the diving department for them. Ian and Kenzie make their way into Maria's room, while Jax stands at the door holding it open. Once inside, they both can hear hissing sounds coming from the air vents. That lets them know the alarms are being tripped. Now they both lie down on the floor and wait for Maria to arrive.

Chapter 7

Long Sleep?

"How long are we going to have to wait for Maria? I mean, I doubt we are anywhere close to the city, so it will take her some time to get there and back. Not to mention the time she is going to need to do whatever it is she is going there to do in the first place," Brayden asks Mason.

"To be honest with you all, I have not put much thought into Maria's time away from here. I guess we will all find out together," Mason answers Brayden's question. It may not have been the answer he was looking for, but that was all Mason was going to share with anyone.

"So, are we just supposed to all stay crammed in this room until Maria comes back?" Brayden is asking yet another question.

"I suppose that we all can't stay in here, so how about the two of you," Mason says to Maclaine and Garrett, "take the other two guests back down to their holding cells. This way I won't have to wonder where they are since I know Kayla will be asleep until Maria awakens her when she returns," Mason expresses to Garrett and Maclaine.

"And what would you like for us to do, once they are in their cages? Do you have anything for us to do while we wait for Maria?" Garrett asks Mason.

"Do you need me to give you something to do, or can you manage to figure out something to do on your own?" Mason gives a snide remark.

"No, Sir, I believe we can find something productive to do," Maclaine answers Mason this time.

Mason turns and walks out of the room, leaving the two of them to get Brayden and Connor down to the holding cells without incident. Mason takes a stroll down to the control room to see if there has been any word from Maria, or anything else that needs his attention.

***

Once Mason leaves the room, Garrett and Maclaine do as they are told and somewhat lead Brayden and Connor back down to the holding cells. They all know that it is just a show. They have to keep up the pretenses where Mason is concerned. They all know that if Mason were to find out the truth about them all working together, he would have them all locked up and not even near each other.

"Come on you two, let's go ahead and get a move on," Maclaine says to the group. "We might as well play the part Mason is expecting us to play."

"Awesome! Let's go down to the dark and empty cells, the ones that are down in the basement of this creepy building. I mean, what other kind of fun could we get into?" Brandon says out loud to anyone who is listening.

"You know we have no options here. If we don't take you to your cells, Mason will surely know that we failed to do such a simple task. And you and I know what happened to the last person that couldn't take someone down to the cells, don't you Maclaine?" Garrett asks.

"Alright, you made your point, Garrett. We will take them down to the cells as Mason has instructed. Now, once we make it down to the pitch-black cells, there is no telling what we can do. Do you get my drift?" Maclaine answers Garrett's question.

"I'm pretty sure I know what you are referring to. You don't have to be a rocket scientist to figure that out." Now it's Connor who is speaking for the first time in about thirty minutes.

"Come on, let's just start moving out of this room. If you don't mind, I have spent enough time in here than I can take today," Garrett spouts out to the group.

"Then why don't you lead the way? The way to our torture chambers," Brayden remarks back to Garrett.

"First of all, you both know that the cells are not torture chambers. Second, you both know that if we don't get down there soon, Mason is sure to send other guards here to find out what is taking so long. Is that what any of you want?" Maclaine straight forward tells the group the truth.

"No, you are right. We need to get down to the cells meant for us. But we need to get going. We have already spent too much time discussing our situation as it is," Connor tells the team.

After Connor speaks, they all step up and make their way to the door of the bedroom. They make their way out of the room and down the hallway to the elevator. They know Mason has cameras on each floor. They also know that once they are in the basement, they will not have to worry about Mason being able to see or hear them with those cameras since it is pitch-black, and there aren't any audio devices.

Garrett reaches out to press the call button for the elevator, but before he can make it to the button, it has already turned red. The red light indicated that the button had already been pressed.

"Maclaine, is there a call button over on your side of the elevator?" Garrett asks Maclaine in the hopes of solving this mystery.

"No, there are no buttons on this side of the elevator. Why are you asking?" Maclaine questions Garrett.

But before Garrett can reply to Maclaine, he looks back at Connor and Brayden. The two of them were laughing, pretty much at Garrett's expense. "So, just what do you two find so funny?" Garrett asks.

Brayden looked over at Connor before coming clean with Garrett. "It was Connor that pressed the elevator call button. Remember, he can move things with his mind," Brayden confesses to Garrett.

"Why didn't you say so from the beginning? Why do you think you have to make a joke about everything?" Before Garrett could go any farther with their scolding, the elevator decides to show up. As the elevator makes its stop on their floor, the doors open, welcoming them all to climb aboard.

The four of them decide to take the elevator up on its offer and climb inside her empty belly. They are all shuffling around the elevator as the door closes. Once the door is closed and sealed, again Connor has already pressed the button for the basement.

"Stop doing that, Connor!" Garrett bursts out with anger.

"Sorry. I didn't see any harm in pressing a button while being in the elevator. I will make sure I contain myself by just trying to bring down buildings," Connor expresses back to Garrett's comment.

"No need to bring down the building. It's only an elevator ride down a few floors, and we will be fine," Maclaine tries to ease the tension in the elevator, which Connor caused by pressing the button on the elevator with his mind and not his finger. That is what upset Garrett the most. Garrett seems to be over whatever had him upset in the first place, now.

They continue on the elevator ride in silence until they reach the basement. As the door begins to open, Connor has something to say.

"Garrett, I would like to apologize for the way I acted a few minutes ago. I've had these powers for as long as I can remember, and I was only allowed to use them when I was alone. I was scared that if mom, I mean those people that were pretending to be our parents, or even if Kenzie, saw me, and any of them found out what I could do, they would all hate me. Or at least I thought they would treat me differently, just because I am not like them. Then I got to go to that amazing school and was able to use my powers all the time, so sometimes it's hard not to use them now. Do you know what I'm talking about?" Connor apologizes to Garett in a long way.

"I get it, Connor, that's why I have already let it go. Thank you for being as grown up as you are with your apology. When a person can find it deep within themselves and are able to admit their faults, it shows the kind of man they are. And you are going to grow up to be a very good man someday, young Connor," Garrett expresses to Connor.

"Thank you, Garrett. I do appreciate that," Connor replies to Garrett.

"If you two are finished, can we please get off this elevator? I'm not sure how many more times I can stick my arm out to keep this door from closing," Brayden speaks up to express his boredom with the whole situation.

"Yes, we are complete," Garrett responds to Brayden.

"What do you mean, you are 'complete'?" Brayden inquires.

"That is something special to me, from a group of which I am a member. That is what we say to each other when we have something to work out between two parties or less. When we have said all we want to say, or need to say, we say we are complete. That ends the conversation one might have for the other. Does that satisfy your need to know everything, Brayden?"

Brayden, Connor, Garrett, and Maclaine make their exit out of the belly of the elevator onto the basement floor. Of course, they walk into a pitch-black room once the door to the elevator closes.

"Make sure you grab a pair of night-vision goggles. I almost forgot how dark it is down here in the cells," Garrett tells everyone as they make their way from the elevator.

As they all exit the elevator, they grab a pair of night-vision glasses that are waiting for them. They each place the glasses on their faces, and all of a sudden, they can see. They are all able to see all the empty cells there in the basement. The basement looks like a large metal caged maze. There are so many ways to go to reach each cage. Brayden and Connor wouldn't have ever known about the intricate details of the room itself if it wasn't for them having access to the goggles.

"So, how long are we going to have to stay in the cage this time?" Brayden asks either Garrett or Maclaine. He doesn't care who answers.

"Not sure. I guess you will be down here until Maria gets back," Garrett answers Brayden.

"That could be two days to a week! You all know how Maria is. She can be quick, or she can take her time if she wants," Brayden replies to Garrett.

"Don't be so overdramatic, Brayden. Maria is not going to leave us here long with Mason, not without her being here herself," Maclaine answers Brayden this time. Maclaine knows Maria better than anyone here, so if he says she won't be long, he means it.

Brayden and Connor take their places in their basement prisons. As they both enter their own private cell, Garrett locks the doors behind them. Now with their cell door locked, Brayden and Connor both move to the makeshift bed hanging from one side of the cell wall.

"Well, I guess we will leave you both to rest for the night. We will come and get you when Maria returns, or if Mason asks for you sooner," Maclaine tells the two jailbirds, which is the only thing you can call them with them sitting in their cells.

Maclaine and Garrett both turn and say their goodbyes to Brayden and Connor, then head towards the elevator. On their way, they take off their night-vision goggles and place them in the bin next to the elevator doors. Even though they had removed and returned their goggles, they let Brayden and Connor keep theirs for the night. Garrett and Maclaine know they would never be caught with them, so they have nothing to worry about.

Garrett and Maclaine step into the elevator once it arrives down to the basement. They both head up two floors, which is where their sleeping quarters are located. As the elevator reaches their floor, the door opens, and they both exit. As they exit the elevator, they seem to be going in different directions, so they bid each other goodnight, and walk in their respective directions to their sleeping quarters.

****

"Okay, Connor, now that they are gone, what do you want to do? You have to have something that's been on your mind," Brayden asks Connor.

"I don't know. I have not had time to think about anything that didn't involve doing what Mason wants us to do. But I'm sure you have something on your mind, don't you?"

"Well, I guess you could say I have an idea, but only if you are up to it."

"It depends on what it is, and what do we have to do to complete your idea?"

"I have a few ideas actually. But I am going to need you to get us out of these cages first. Do you think you can do that?"

"I think I should be able to, now that I have these night vision goggles. I should be able to focus on the door locks and unlock them. Will that work for you?"

"Yes, that will be perfect. Do you think you can do it now?"

"Did you hear that?"

"Hear what?"

"The click of our door locks to our cells opening."

"Boy, you are not only quick, but you are very good. You must have been training at the school when none of us saw you."

"You would be surprised by the things I have learned at the school. I can do things I never thought possible until the teachers showed me the proper way to focus my energy on my powers. Once they showed me how to use my powers, it all became so simple."

"What do you mean so simple?"

"Sorry, I'm not going to bore you with all the mind techniques and details of my training. But I can say that it will come in handy with whatever you have in mind."

Brayden pushes his door open, still surprised that it is actually open and by Connor himself. As he walks past Connor's cell, before he can open his door for him, Connor is pushing his door open with his mind, of course. "Hey, you need to be a bit more careful when using your powers. This door could have knocked me out."

"Sorry, Brayden. I did not expect you to come and open my unlocked door for me. You are such a gentleman," Connor bursts out laughing at Brayden.

"That's not funny, Connor. You really could have hurt me if I didn't have such quick reflexes," Brayden says while trying to mend his ego.

"I was just joking. You know that, right? The part about you being a gentleman. I know you were just being nice. Now that we have all of that behind us, what do you have in mind for our escape?"

"I'm afraid if I tell you, you will not want to help me," Brayden is finally beginning to be honest with Connor.

"Help you with what, Brayden?"

"Fine, I want us to make our way back to the room we were in before. You know, the one that is beside Kayla's room."

"Why in the world would you be willing to risk both our lives to go back to that room since we will be back in there tomorrow? And this better be good and the truth or I'm not going," Connor stands his moral ground.

"I need to get back in that room because I need to make contact with Kayla. I need to explain everything that's happening to her. She does not know she is unable to wake up on her own. She is stuck in a long sleep expecting me to come back by now, and I'm sure she thinks I'm hours late. Someone needs to let her in on what's going on, don't you agree?"

"You are right. Kayla can't stay all night like that. That sounds like it could cause a normal person to go crazy. I may not know Kayla, but I know I don't want her to go crazy," Connor replies to Brayden with a deep sadness in his voice. He almost sounds as if he may be crying, just at the thought of Kayla going crazy.

"Connor, are you alright? You sound like you are getting a little choked up over there."

"I'm fine, but what are we doing just standing around here? We need to get up to that room, and you need to connect with Kayla if we are going to be able to save her. Do you understand how important this mission is right now?" Connor tells Brayden, even though this has been Brayden's idea from the get-go.

"Then, how about you come out of your cell, and let's make our way up to Kayla's floor, so we can do whatever we can to save her?"

"Let's go then. Why are you wanting?"

"Hey, slow down there, Connor. We are both going to the same place, but there are going to be some obstacles we will have to get through using your powers," Brayden explains a small part of the dangers they will face that only Connor can fix.

"What are you talking about? What am I going to have to do? Please don't say I have to hurt anyone because you can do that on your own," Connor asks to get clarification on his part of this mission.

"I hope you don't have to hurt anyone, but do you remember where the cameras are in the hallway? Because those are what I will need you to move. That way we will not be seen walking the halls. Do you think you can do that?"

"I think I can move the cameras. We need to go slow because I do not remember where all the cameras are, at least not from the elevator to the room," Connor admits to Brayden.

"Don't worry, we are going to go as slow as possible, so we don't draw attention to ourselves, but also to give you the opportunity to move the cameras."

"Okay, I am ready then. Let's get on with our mission," Connor tells Brayden.

With Connor's orders, Brayden tells him to follow where he goes. Brayden leads them to the elevator. Once they make it to the only elevator in or out of the basement, Connor presses the elevator call button, while Brayden goes to put their night vision glasses in the bin with all the other ones. Just as Brayden drops the last pair of glasses in the bin, the elevator finds its stop in the basement. Just as quickly as the elevator found its floor, the door opened. It's as if it is begging the two of them to step inside. Their adventure awaits.

Chapter 8

Cameras?

As they both lie on Maria's bedroom floor, they hear the door to her room close. Neither Ian nor Kenzie knows if Jax closed the door because Maria's here, or if it just slipped out of his grasp. They didn't have to say anything to each other to both agree it is best to assume Maria is here, and Jax has gone to hide from her.

A few seconds later, the door clicks to its unlocked position, the door swings open, and there stands Maria. As she is standing there, she has a look of wonder shoot across her face when she notices two people lying on her floor. Now the wonder-struck look is not because there are two people on her floor but the outfits they are wearing. *Why would anyone wear scuba tanks to break into someone's room?* Maria thinks to herself.

So we could stay awake until you got home, so you could see who broke into your room. This way we can catch you, instead of you catching us and taking us away like you did my brother, Connor, and Brayden, Kenzie thinks back to Maria after making sure Ian was looped in.

After Kenzie's words sink in with Maria, she and Ian begin to stand up off her floor. They both look like they are ready to go treasure hunting in the Hudson River in New York.

"So, what exactly does your attire have to do with you being awake right now?" Maria asks either of them out loud.

"Why don't you let me answer that for you, Maria?" Jax says as he enters her living quarters. "Their outfits are thanks to me. I got those for them to make sure they were able to stay awake through any of your traps. You see, the oxygen in the tanks allowed them to be in your room and breathe, but not having to breathe your toxic air in your room. That is how they are awake now, and **you** are caught instead of them. I figured you would love a good act, like the one you gave us back here at the school. You remember, when you were talking through a speakerphone in the lobby area," Jax finishes as he shuts Maria's living quarter's door behind him and makes sure the lights are on.

"So, are you going to make sure no more of your traps go off while we are in here at least? Or do we need to move this meeting to another room which we have control over?" Ian asks Maria.

"No, we can stay in my room. I will not try any tricks on the three of you. To be honest, I believe it is about time that we all had a conversation about what is going on. Don't you all agree?"

Jax moves away from the door and makes his way closer to Ian and Kenzie. Maria steps aside to allow Jax to get by. He could tell by her subtle movements that she is telling the truth to them.

"Please, have a seat and make yourselves comfortable. I think the questions you have for me will be answered by what I have to tell you all first. So if you will allow me to explain myself, and a few other things to you as well, you may see things a little differently."

"That's fine, Maria, you can start this meeting, but if we don't like what we hear, we will stop you. Remember, there is plenty we already know, so if you try to lie to us, we will know," Jax answers Maria with his own stipulations.

Maria accepts the additional stipulations and makes a promise she will not lie to them. She expresses she does not need to lie anymore because she is counting on their help. Maria takes a stand in front of Jax, Ian, and Kenzie to begin explaining things from her point of view.

***

The elevator door closes, which lets them both know that there is no turning back now. Brayden and Connor's mission has now begun, and they both know they have to complete it, for Kayla's sake.

"What do we do if there are people outside the elevator when the door opens?" Connor asks Brayden.

"First of all, let's not think negative thoughts before we even begin to start our mission. Do you know that if you think of bad things, they end up happening? So, let's keep our thoughts on a positive level from now on. Think good thoughts," Brayden tells Connor.

"Sorry, I didn't know just..." and Connor gets cut off.

"What are you doing? I said no bad thoughts, which includes just talking about them. Do you get it now?" Brandon snaps at Connor after cutting him off in mid-sentence.

"Okay, you don't have to be so rude about it," Connor replies.

Just as Connor finishes his sentence this time, the elevator comes to a stop on their new floor they are needing. They both hold their breath and stand next to the wall of the elevator, just in case someone else is there. The door opens to give them access to the floor. Brayden peeks his head around the corner of the open door, to make sure the coast is clear, which it is.

"Okay, we are clear to exit this elevator. Now, follow me and stay close so I can point out the cameras to you. But if you see them before I can point them out to you, please go ahead and take charge and adjust their angles," Brayden tells Connor.

"That works for me because I do know where several of the cameras are located."

"Then let's get this mission started as we don't have much time to waste."

With Brayden's words of wisdom, he exits the elevator while motioning for Connor to follow him. Connor takes his lead from Brayden and exits the elevator behind him. Just as Connor passes through the elevator door, it begins to close.

"I think we need to move away from this area since the elevator could just sit here, or it could be on its way down to another floor to pick up someone who has called for it. Either way, I think moving is our best option," Connor advises Brayden of their current situation.

"Okay, then let's make sure we move down the hall while hugging this side of the wall. Then if we see someone or a camera, you can move its view and I'll..."

"Let's play the next part by ear. There is too much at risk to only depend on you to take care of others we may run into. In other words, what I am saying is that if we come across someone, I will do my best to help, but I will not kill anyone."

"That sounds like a fantastic plan, Connor. You know I would never want to do anything that you are not comfortable with doing."

"I know, and this is a decision I have made on my own. I want to be as much help as possible for Kayla."

"I agree with you, Connor. Now, let's start down the hallway along this wall. I know there are more than at least two cameras that will be coming up pretty quickly. Are you ready for this?"

"Ready," Connor answers Brayden's question. Just about that time, they come to their first dilemma. Before Brayden can say anything to Connor, he has already turned the camera in the opposite direction.

"Good catch with that camera. I didn't remember seeing it there. I wonder if it's new or if I have just missed it."

"It doesn't matter. It's been moved, so let's keep going to our next stop," Connor tells Brayden.

The two of them continue down the side of the hallway until they reach the second area with multiple cameras. "Why are you stopping?" Connor asks Brayden.

"Because this section of the hall is going to be a bit tricky. You see, there are more than two cameras here. There are six or seven in this zone alone. We are going to have to be very careful here. If you move the wrong camera at the wrong time, it could set off alarms in the other cameras when they notice the camera has changed."

"So what you are saying is I'm going to have to be not only fast but also accurate," Connor tells Brayden.

"You guessed it. So do you think you can pull this off? Can you turn all the cameras away from us without setting off any alarms?"

"Give me a minute so I can give this zone a good look around," Connor says to Brayden. Once he says what he needs to for Brayden to understand, Connor begins to survey the area he is about to secure. Once he gets all of the information he needs on the zone and the cameras, Connor turns to Brayden to let him know that he can handle the area with no problems that he can foresee. Brayden gives Connor a nod, meaning for him to turn around and get to work.

Connor takes care of the first three cameras and turns them away from their location. Next, he takes the second three cameras and moves them to look in strange directions. Then, just as Connor is going for the last camera, a guard comes around the corner. Connor takes a quick look over to Brayden for some guidance, but Brayden is just standing there looking at the guard as well. Connor knows he is going to get no guidance from Brayden. Connor uses his powers to slam the guard up against the hall wall, fast and hard enough the guard is knocked out cold on the first try from Connor. Then Connor turns the last camera away from them while the unconscious guard lays on the hallway floor.

"What in the world were you thinking just now? He could have walked right past us. Why did you have to knock him out?"

"I didn't have much time to think about what I was going to do in order to move that last camera. I looked at you for instructions, but you were mesmerized by the guard as well you just stood there. Since you were going to be no help, I did what I had to do and made the decision to knock him out quickly, then moved the last camera. So, to be honest with you, I would have to say I did very well without your help. Maybe you can help with the next emergency."

"That's very funny, but what are we going to do with the guard?"

"Make me do everything," Connor says back to Brayden as he uses his powers to move the unconscious guard's body over to their location, which will keep him from being found, for now anyway. "There, is that going to work for you, or would you like me to place him on the ceiling?" Connor says to Brayden jokingly.

"On the floor will be fine. We don't need a random guard falling from the ceiling before we have finished our mission. Wouldn't you agree?" Brayden asks Connor in return.

"Of course, why do you think I chose the former of the two options?"

"Then, since the guard is taken care of, maybe we should continue on our own mission to the room next to Kayla's?" Brayden asks.

"Yes, let's get a move on if we want to make it there and have actual time for you to connect with

Kayla. You know, to let her know what's going on, so she does not go crazy."

With those remarks from Connor, Brayden decides it's time for them to continue their way to the room next to Kayla's. Brayden nudges Connor from their hiding spot, now that the cameras and the guard are all taken care of, and leads them down the hall. This time they don't have cameras to worry about, but they still move at a slow pace, just in case there are more cameras of which they may not be aware. And if there are any new guard's surprises, Brandon won't be so shocked this time and will be ready to help young Connor.

They both continue alongside the wall slowly. Suddenly, Brayden notices a couple of cameras on the ceiling. He signals to Connor and points at the cameras for him to move, so they won't be seen. Connor moves the two cameras, and again the coast is clear. They continue on their journey to the room next to Kayla's room. They are still unaware if there are any more cameras or stray guards.

Finally, they both can see the door to the room next to Kayla's. Their first instinct is to run as fast as they can to that door, and if it's locked, then Connor can open it. But they both choose not to go with their first thoughts and decide to continue nice and slow, the same way they have been going. It's a good thing, too, because just before they were going to cross the hall, Connor noticed a few new cameras, which stopped Brayden from moving forward and ruining all of their hard work they have done up to this part. Once Brayden was on the same track as Connor, he let Connor adjust the three remaining cameras between them and the room they needed to access.

Now that the cameras are all taken care of by Connor, the boys are prepared to make a run to the bedroom door. Unfortunately, they are stopped in their tracks again. This time it's by another guard making his rounds. Connor was about to use his powers on the unsuspecting guard, but before he could, Brayden stepped out from their hiding spot and put the guard in a sleeper hold. It's an old wrestling move to make someone fall asleep during a match without hurting them. This move seems to be working on the guard. His eyes are closing, and he has not been able to utter a single word for help. The next thing they both know is that the guard is asleep. Now that he is asleep, Brayden pulls the guard over to their location close to the wall and lays him down behind the plants and chairs they are using for cover.

Once Brayden and Connor have the sleeping guard securely bound, they feel they are in the clear to make a dash for the room next to Kayla's room. They make their quick passage across the hall to the room door, the one they have been working towards this whole time. As they make their way, Connor is already working on the lock, so they will have an easy entry once they make it across the hall.

Because of Connor's pre-lock work, as soon as they make it to the door, the door opens right up for them. As the door opens for them, they both are able to make it inside without any disruptions. Once they made it safely inside the room, they quickly shut the door and lock it back again.

Now that they are in the room they need to be in, the same one they were in before being removed and taken back to their holding cells in the basement, they begin to make sure it's safe, and there is no one there in the room with them. As they both are satisfied that the room is only occupied by the two of them, Connor is glad that they locked the door as soon as they entered.

Being secure and alone in the room they both know all too well, Brayden goes over to the only bed in the room. The same bed he used while he was making contact with Kayla all of the times he tried to breach Kayla's defenses, and that last time when he was actually able to make contact with her. That was the time they all were pretending to be asleep, so Brayden could make that meet and greet so smoothly. Which it did, go smoothly. Now Brayden is going to have to make contact with Kayla again, and this time fill her in on the fact that she is stuck asleep until Maria comes back from the school to release her. That is going to be one difficult moment between Kayla and Brayden.

As much as Brayden is dreading this conversation with Kayla, he knows it's the right thing to do. Brayden climbs onto the bed and lays back, allowing his head to hit the pillow. He closes his eyes and begins to reach out with his mind to Kayla's mind. But before he can make any connection, he is interrupted.

"Hey, Brayden? What do you want me to do while you are with Kayla?" Connor asks for instructions from Brayden.

"How about you watch the door but remain completely quiet? This way, if any guards walk by checking locks, we will be covered. Remember, there are two knocked out guards that could regain consciousness at any time and let everyone else know that we are on the loose, and we caused them to pass out and tied up," Brayden explains to Connor.

"Well, to be on the safe side, the guard I took out never saw either of us before I used my powers to knock him out. So he won't be able to say who did that to him. Now, your guard is a completely different story. He got a good look at you as you rushed him to put him into the sleeper hold. So he would be the only person that could ID us," Connor clarifies.

"This is not the time to be separating what we did as a team. I asked you to watch the door and hold anyone that tries to come in here back until we complete our mission. Is that understood?"

"Yes, Sir, that is something I can do. I won't let you down."

"Good, now let me try and make a connection with Kayla."

With Connor's promise to keep them safe, Brayden lies back down on the bed. Once he is comfortable on the bed, he begins again to stretch his mind to Kayla's. Brayden has to try several times before Kayla will let him in.

"Hello? Kayla, are you here? It's me, Brayden. We have some things to talk about," Brayden is thinking in Kayla's mind.

"Yes, Brayden, I'm here. Where else would I be? Remember this is my mind, so it would be hard for me to escape my own mind, wouldn't it?" Kayla tells Brayden.

"Well, I am glad you are here with me because we have a lot to go over and a very short time to go over it all."

"Then I guess you better get started with telling me what you need to tell me."

Chapter 9

Truth?

"I need you all to understand one thing. I did not ask for this mission, nor did I even feel I could do it. There were so many more cunning people than I was back then. But one does not refuse Chancellor Billie June. Isn't that right, Ian? Don't worry. I'm the only person that knows you were there when I was, basically forced to be, the replacement spy in Mason's group," Maria starts with her explanation.

"You mean you could see me while Junior was walking me through another memory?" Ian asks Maria.

"Yes, Ian, I could see you, but not this Junior person you are referring to. That will have to be something we clear up during this release of information," Maria replies.

"We will see as we move forward. First, let's test your complete honesty. Why don't you tell us all exactly why you were forced to be the replacement spy?" Ian is now forcing Maria's hand.

"Just so you know, Ian could have already told everyone this information. But like I said in the beginning, I will not lie or hold anything from any of you. I just hope you are prepared to deal with all of the aftermath. Are you, Ian?" Maria throws the ball back in Ian's court to see how far his courage will take him.

Without a shutter, Ian answers, "Yes, I am prepared to be here for my friends," with a powerful response to Maria.

"Then let's proceed, shall we?"

"Please continue," this time it's Kenzie giving the orders.

"If you insist. Years ago, I was called to the head of the Believers', at that time, office. At the time, I did not know why I was being called in, but when I arrived and Clint was there, I had an idea why. I knew for sure when your parents were not there," Maria says as she looks at Kenzie.

"What do my parents have to do with any of this? I know my parents gave my brother and me away to that horrible couple Jerry and Delores, for doing something for Mason. No one ever told us about our real parents until a few months ago. So why would my parents be at some meeting with you anyway?" Kenzie questions Maria.

"I'm sure Ian's friend Junior told him the story while they were watching me. So why don't you ask him to tell you?"

"No, Maria. I don't want to find out about my real parents from a story that was told to Ian when I can get the whole story from someone who lived it. Now start talking," Kenzie expresses her feelings to Maria.

"If that is what you wish, then I have no problem telling you. I believe you are not only old enough but also strong enough to hear the facts about your parents' disappearance," Maria starts her explanation of what Kenzie's real parents have to do with all of this.

"What do you mean 'disappearance'? I always figured my real parents just left after giving us away to the Greens. So where are they now? Where are Connor and my real parents?" Kenzie asks Maria for answers.

"I'm sorry, Kenzie, but that is a difficult question that I cannot answer. I only know the story I was told that night Ian was there. It was put in the form of a memory for him. Once the Greens erased your parents' memories and Mason took you two, there wasn't anything discussed about where your parents went. I'm sorry, I really wish I could tell you more about them or where they could be today, but I can't tell you what I don't know. You can even search my mind if you would like. I have no objections or anything to hide from you. I told you in the beginning that I would not lie to either of you, and I meant that," Maria expresses to Kenzie and Ian, but more to Kenzie.

"No, I don't need to search your mind to know you are telling the truth. I can already feel it in your words," Kenzie replies to Maria.

"Then you also know how sorry I am for all of this. I did not find out about you and Connor until later that evening. But there is so much more we need to go over, but not now. I need to return to where I was before I came here. And it's not just for my sake, but for five other people who are depending on me. Do you mind if we come back to this later?" Maria asks of Kenzie.

"No, that's fine. I agree that we need to focus on the others and what we need to know to help them," Kenzie agrees with Maria.

"Well, I do wish it were that simple, but it is way more complicated than that. I have people on both sides that I'm watching. But don't get me wrong, when I say both sides, it's because they are all on my side. They all, but one, know the truth about me and my mission," Maria explains.

"Then how can someone be on your side if they don't know you're there to help them? Wouldn't they assume you are with Mason?" Ian asks the questions at the same time.

"Yes they do, but with the help of the others, they will be able to fill her in before she is awaked again," Maria replies in a rush.

"You just said 'her' and 'she', so are you talking about Kayla? And don't lie to me," Ian begs Maria.

"Yes, Ian, Kayla is one of the people that I am looking out for, and she is the only one that does not know I'm helping her. But she will know soon enough. Just as soon as I get back, Brayden will be able to dream-walk Kayla and explain everything to her before she wakes up," Maria fills in with a bit more of her plans.

"So Connor and Brayden are safe as well? I mean, we already know you have taken them with you from here," Kenzie requests of Maria, mainly to hear about Connor.

"Yes, Kenzie, Connor is safe. He has always been safe with me. I'm sure the way that he and Brayden left with me left you with doubts that they were safe, but I had to play a role in front of Mason's guards and continue that same role once we arrived at his compound in Woodville. They are about two and a half hours northeast of us, here in Houston, in a large warehouse at the edge of the city. To be honest, the city of Woodville is not very big so anyone could find Mason's compound if they just knew exactly they were looking for," Maria gives in great detail, not only of Mason's location but also of his hideout.

"What is the reason we can't go out there when you go?" Ian asks in concern for Kayla.

"Because there are things that Mason must go through and experience in order to stop this from becoming a historical loop. If you understand what I mean," Maria reveals to everyone.

"Well, if anyone in this room understands time and history loops, it will be Ian. Or have you forgotten just what Ian is capable of?" Jax finally speaks.

"No, I remember all too well what Ian can do. That is why I am here, and that is the exact reason Mason wants Ian. Mason thinks I have caught you, Ian, in my room. That is the reason you cannot go storming Mason's compound. Not right now anyway. If he has you, then the others are no longer of value to him, so there is no telling what he could do to them. That is why we must wait for the right moment before bringing you out to Woodville," Maria is practically begging Jax, Ian, and Kenzie to wait. All Maria can do is nod at them and hope it's enough for them to understand the severity of her words and that they will respect them.

"Relax, Maria. We can tell how important it is for us to stay clear of Mason's compound for the time being. Now, how long are you expecting all of us to continue waiting? You know we are going to get Kayla, Connor, and Brayden and bring them home. That is the only way we can figure out a way to bring Kayla back to our timeline for Ian." Kenzie is now expressing her feelings and asking questions the other two were thinking.

"It's not an exact science. It's kind of hard to give you an exact time. You understand what I'm talking about, don't you, Jax?"

"Yes, I do, and so do Ian and Kenzie. You do not have to treat them like children considering this was their plan to catch you instead of you catching them. Meaning they can understand exactly what you are asking of us."

"I'm sorry, you two. It was not my intention to make you think I thought any less of you. I know how smart you both are, and together you are a powerful duo. But I think you have already figured this out for yourselves, yes?"

"You could say we have felt stronger together than when we try things on our own. Now, as far as being very powerful together, that's new to us both," Ian replies to Maria's comment.

"I can assure you both when you use your powers together, there is not much you can't accomplish. I can also tell you that Mason knows this as well about you two. So, this is another reason for you both to stay away for now."

"Yes, we understand that we need to stay away for now, but you also have not told us exactly when we will be able to actually go out to Mason's compound. Are we expected to wait a day or two? What is the magic number of days you are talking about?" Ian soothes Maria's worries that they will not do anything hasty.

"I can't be one hundred percent correct, down to the date and time, but I can say that everything will happen within the coming week."

"A WEEK? No one ever said we were going to have to wait a week. That is an unacceptable timeline you are offering. You have to shorten this week down to a day or so, or we will storm Mason's compound on our own to search for Kayla, Connor, and Brayden without your help. I hope you understand that I mean business. I have not searched this long for Kayla, and come this close, to wait a week to go and help her," Ian expresses his feelings towards Maria's suggestion.

"I'm sorry to you all, but there is nothing I can do to ensure your window of opportunity can be moved any closer to seven days."

"What if we could do something to make sure the date we want is the date we create? Would you be okay with that?" Ian asks Maria.

"Are you sure that is something the two of you can actually do? If that is something you can pull off, then I say yes," Maria answers.

"Perfect! Then we will let you know when we decide on the exact date and time. I can assure you that it will be within the next two days, so be prepared. Also, you may want to let the others know. That way, they will be prepared as well," Ian instructs Maria.

"That sounds fantastic. I will go ahead and make my way back to Woodville. I need an excuse as to why I don't have anyone with me or how they could have escaped my room. But not to worry, I will be able to come up with something Mason will believe. That will not be my first time to have to lie to Mason," Maria expresses to Jax, Ian, and Kenzie.

"Great, then you need to go and head back and deal with Mason. He must not suspect anything that is going on with us. I know you understand the importance of all of this," Ian replies to Maria.

"Yes, I understand. I will make sure to be discrete to where Mason does not know what he is getting into," Maria answers Ian.

With that, Maria took the hint and exited out of her room. Maria walks down to the elevator, as her bedroom door shuts behind her. Just as Mara presses the call button for the elevator, the doors open as if the elevator was already waiting on her floor. Now that the door is open, Maria climbs aboard the elevator, presses the button for the first floor, and just like that, she is gone.

Meanwhile, back in Maria's room, Jax, Ian, and Kenzie are discussing everything they learned from Maria. Some things they already suspected, while other information left them speechless.

Once they finish discussing everything Maria had told them, they begin to make plans on what Ian and Kenzie will be able to do together that can speed up the timeline from a week to just two days. Neither of them can think of anything they can do to speed up the process. Then the next thing Ian and Jax hear is Kenzie saying something that makes them both stop and think. Kenzie is very smart, and the school she went to proves it.

"What did you just say, Kenzie?" Ian asks.

"I have an idea," Kenzie replies.

"About what we can do together" How do you know that we can do what you are about to suggest?" Ian again replies to Kenzie.

"I just have a feeling, guess you could say. Why are you asking about my idea? I thought you trusted me by now," Kenzie responds to Ian's remarks.

"I do trust you, Kenzie. I'm just not fully used to having someone helping me nor someone taking charge when needed. It's an odd feeling, but a good feeling at the same time. It's nice to have someone to have my back. I've always been used to Kayla being that person. That's the only reason it feels odd. I know you will be perfect to have my back, just like I hope you know I will be perfectly fine covering your back as well. I won't let anything happen to you, or Connor, once we are in the compound."

"Thank you, Ian, that means a lot to me. Your trust, that is, because you know I will always be at your side, no matter what. No matter what is thrown our way, we will both be covered."

"I believe you. Now we need to figure out the best day and time to go to Mason's compound. Even harder than that, how can we convince someone in the compound to move their final date up two days."

"Don't worry, Ian, I have all of that already figured out. When the time is right, I will tell you everything. But right now, I need you thinking about what we are going to do once I teleport us to the compound. Before you ask, yes, I will teleport us to the compound, so our travel time is cut way down. This way, we will have a little extra time to grab Kayla since my power will freeze everyone when we get there. We will be in their compound before they even know we are there."

Chapter 10

Girls' Day Out?

Garrett is having a hard time sleeping tonight. He has too much on his mind with everything going on with Maria and her sudden departure. Just as Garrett was beginning to believe her as someone on his side, she goes and does this. All he can do is toss and turn in his bed so much he rolls right out of his bed and onto the hard concrete floor. With that thump on the floor by his body, he jumps up and decides to take a long walk because that's just maybe what he needs to catch some "Z's".

So Garrett makes his way over to his dresser. He figures a clean set of clothes would be best for him this evening, being wide awake. His pajama shorts will not do because he knows there is no rhyme or reason who you may run into while on a nighttime walk alone.

Once Garrett was presentable to whom he may run into, he decided to make his way out of his room. He grabs the doorknob and freezes for just a minute. He is remembering the first time he and Kayla had ahold of the other side of the door now.

Kayla felt a tug as she pushed on the door of his room, then all of sudden the door flew open and she fell in the arms of Garrett. All he can remember is looking into her eyes. As of that moment, Garrett does not see any fear, scared, or loneliness in her eyes. Garrett felt a connection in her eyes. He felt a connection with Kayla in that very short moment.

Garrett went and opened his bedroom door, and no surprise, Kayla was not on the other side of the door ready to fall into his arms.

As his door was closing, he went ahead and took a walk out of his room and began his way down the non-descript hallway that leads to the entrance waiting room to Mason's hideout. The entrance waiting room where Kayla and Mason watched Maria bring in her new guests Brayden and Connor. That was the first day both of them became 'guests' at the compound.

Garrett continued his walk down his hallway until he reached the sitting areas in the front of the compound entrance. He is happy that no one is taking advantage of the area, and it is empty at this time of night. Since the area is clear, Garrett makes his way across the empty sitting area to the hall leading to the hub of the compound.

***

Maclaine is having a rough time sleeping as well and decides that he needs to go for a long walk to clear his mind. He crawls out of his bed and as soon as both of his feet hit the floor, he shoots up and makes his way to the restroom. Once he has finished using the restroom, he makes his way to his clean clothes. He feels he needs to be dressed in clean clothes, even for a walk. Seems like he has a lot in common with Garrett than he knows, yet.

Maclaine grabs his bedroom doorknob, gives it a twist, and pulls his bedroom door open. He takes a step through the open door, then closing it behind him. Once his door is secure, he begins his walk down one of the corridors next to his bedroom. Maclaine's quarters are much different than Garrett's, of course, neither of them knows where the other's sleeping quarters are located. Maclaine continues down the hallway just off his bedroom door. He has no destination in mind, except a long walk to clear his head, so he can get some real sleep tonight. He knows he needs to just walk down as many halls as he needs until he is able to go back to his room and go back to bed and actually get some sleep.

Maclaine continues down the corridor to the end where he has to make a turn to the left. Turning left is going to take Maclaine past the control center. He knows he will pass by the elevators that go down to the basement where Connor and Brayden are being housed at the moment. He has not made any decisions as to if he is going to go down and check on them by the time he gets to the elevators.

Maclaine continues his walking path down the second hallway, trying to think of absolutely nothing, wanting to keep a clear mind. He is taking this walk to ease his thoughts, just so he can get to bed and get some real sleep for once. He continues down his current hallway, until he notices he is passing the control center. "Wow, that was fast. I didn't think I would make it this far this fast," Maclaine says out loud. As he looks down at his watch, he also notices over twenty minutes have passed since he began his walk into the void of nothingness.

Maclaine takes a look in the control center window to see if anything is happening out in the compound besides him being unable to sleep. As he is peering through the window, the guards that are supposed to be watching the monitors look as if they just might be asleep. That tells Maclaine that it must be a very slow night indeed since the guards are not keeping an eye on the entire compound tonight.

Maclaine chooses to continue his walk. He still has been unsuccessful in clearing his mind to be able to sleep like the guards at the control center who are doing it so well. He continues along the hallway, down towards the elevators which lead down to Brayden and Connor in the basement cells. Maclaine makes his way to the elevators, as for him they are just a middle stopping point for his late-night walk. As soon as he walks up to the elevators, he stops dead in his tracks. "What are you doing here?"

***

Garrett makes his way across the empty sitting room, to the hall that leads to the hub of the compound. He is not sure what that includes, as he has never been past the elevators. These are the same elevators that lead down to the basement, to the place where Brayden and Connor are being forced to reside while they are guests in Mason's compound.

Garrett continues his walk, trying to clear his mind so he can fall asleep. He is beginning to make his way to the elevators. Garrett has an idea of how long it will take him to get there. So he takes his time walking at a slow pace to try and burn up a little more time. He figures the more time that passes, the quicker he can go back to bed. As Garrett clears a corner in the hallway, he stops dead in his tracks. "What exactly are you doing here in the middle of the night? I'm asking first."

***

"I couldn't sleep, so I thought I would take a walk to clear my head. Now, what are you doing here?" Maclaine asks Garrett, who is just standing in front of him, with a stunned look on his face.

"To be honest, I couldn't sleep either and had the same idea as you. I'd walk around this enormous compound until my mind was completely empty of anything not worth thinking about, so I can go to bed and get some sleep," Garrett answers Maclaine's question.

"It's a bit of a coincidence that neither of us can sleep tonight and then both go for a walk at the exact same time, don't you think?" Maclaine asks Garrett.

"Why don't you get to what you are really wanting to say to me right now?" Garrett fires back at Maclaine.

"I'm just saying it's a bit odd for both of us to be up at the same time in the middle of the night, the day before we have a very important mission to complete. Don't tell me you are not thinking the same thing right now, or that this has been set up in some way?" Maclaine inquires to Garrett.

"Well, if this is a setup, then are **we** being set up, or are we here to catch the others breaking the rules?"

"Now that is something I have not even thought about. I assumed someone was wanting us to meet for some reason."

"I'm not sure what good that could do for anyone unless they are listening to our conversation. The last I checked none of these cameras have audio, only video. So if someone is listening to us, they will have to be close by."

After Garrett finishes his statement, the two of them begin to laugh out loud. Neither of them takes it seriously that someone would actually try and follow them to listen to their conversation. For one, Mason knows that either of them would be able to pick up on anyone following them. But just as quickly as they started laughing, they stopped.

"Okay, now what is the matter? Why did you stop laughing?" Garrett asks Maclaine.

"Well, you know as well as I do that things have changed over the past few weeks. So who is to say Mason hasn't upgraded his security system? You know, with all this new company we have here, he has to suspect some kind of attack from Jax, Ian, and Kenzie."

"How sure are you that Mason actually did those modifications to his entire security system? He has never seemed like the type of person that would be in a hurry to do anything. Do you know what I am talking about? That is a man that thinks about thinking before he even thinks."

"I know what you mean, but for some reason, this just feels different to me."

"Do you think he did the cameras down in the basement? Down there where Brayden and Connor are forced to sleep?"

"I doubt they would have upgraded those. They have always figured the people in the dark would not speak anyway, and just fall asleep."

"Then why don't we go down and bother them for a while, since we are awake and can't sleep anyway? If we have to be awake, then it's only fair that they should be awake with us. Don't you agree?"

"What can it hurt? We are already here at the elevators. Might as well visit our friends down in their holding cells."

"Cool, then let's get a move on it. I have already hit the down button for the elevator. There is no turning back now."

As Garrett finishes his remarks, they wait for the elevator in silence. They don't have to wait long as the elevator seems to already be on their floor. Once the elevator doors open, both of them make their way in. Neither of them mentioned to the other their thoughts of the elevator being on their floor instead of down on the bottom on the basement floor where it should be. Now that they have made their way onto the elevator, Garrett presses the basement button. Maclaine gives him a look that lets Garrett know that the next time, he better be the one pressing any buttons. Garrett did not have time to say anything back to Maclaine, even though he had plenty to say to him.

Once the elevator door opens in the basement, they make their way out of it. Garrett lets

Maclaine go first, just so he wouldn't start more drama in front of Brayden and Connor, who they believe to be locked in their cells, sleeping. But Garrett and Maclaine quickly figure out that they are alone in the basement. Somehow, Brayden and Connor have escaped from their cells, but there is no way they can make it very far from the elevator. Garrett and Maclaine will remain clueless unless they find them before Mason does.

"Now, where do you think they are? How could they break out of their cells? It's pitch black down here, so neither of them can use their gifts," Maclaine rages at Garrett.

"Are you asking me a question or accusing me of something? Because it sounds a bit like an accusation. How am I supposed to know where they are or how they got to wherever they were going now? I have been walking these lovely halls just like you have. So again, let me ask you, do you think I know anything about their escape or whereabouts?" Garrett is seriously asking Maclaine for some clarification on his previous remark.

"I'm sorry to sound like I am accusing you of anything. I am aware we have been together and what you were doing before we met up this evening. It has been the same thing I have been doing myself. I am just really popping out in my head, but my thoughts came out of my mouth before I could stop them. Please accept my apologies. I am so in shock right now that they are not here. Brayden and Connor are going to get us all caught, even before we get a chance to get back in the room next to Kayla's."

"I accept your apology, and I can feel your frustration. I also believe you have answered one of your own questions, 'back to the room next to Kayla's." Do you think they may have gone back there to try to connect with Kayla again? I would not doubt it if they wanted to try to speak to Kayla alone without everyone around to listen, in case Brayden says something out loud while he is connected with her. For what reason, that's another question they can answer when we do find them!"

"Then let's get a move on, the sooner the better if we want to stay out of trouble and be able to complete our mission tomorrow and not tonight."

"I agree with you, Maclaine. We have to make that one of our first locations we check off our list. We should check both rooms to be on the safe side. We need to cover all of our bases until they are found. You lead the way and I'll follow you," is what Garrett suggests to Maclaine.

"Then let's go because we have no time to waste," Maclaine replies to Garrett as he walks past him to the elevator. Now, with Garrett in tow, they board the elevator that has been waiting for them and leave the basement to hunt down their two escapees, Brayden and Connor.

***

"You might want to take a seat, Kayla, as this is not going to be a pleasant meeting we are about to have," Brayden does as Ian does, and speaks out loud and in Kayla's mind so Connor can hear their conversation and know what is said on his side.

Connor watches the door while listening to Brayden. He knows he can do both things at one time. He also knows it's the best way to get information and keep them both safe. Connor is thankful that Brayden is allowing him to listen to his side of their conversation, the one Brayden is having with Kayla with his mind. Connor gets settled for watch duty and is ready for anything that comes his way.

"Kayla, I'm sorry to have to tell you, but I'm not here right now for our regular meeting that is supposed to be happening. Connor and I have broken out of our cells so I could come to speak to you again. You see, after our last visit, Maria received a text and had to make a quick exit. But before she left, Maria did something to you and said to Mason that you would not wake up until her return. None of us are exactly sure how long that will be, so since we do not know Maria's schedule, we wanted to let you know what has been going on. This way if you try to wake up and are unable to, you will know why. Or if you wake up and wonder where I am, you will know that too. Don't lose hope in me. I will get you out of here."

"Who are you? How did you get into my room?" Kayla asks Brayden.

"What? Kayla, don't you remember who I am? It's me, Brayden. We met earlier today. I am friends with your best friend, Ian. Do you know who Ian is?" Brayden asks Kayla.

"Yes, I know Ian. He lives here in my building. We have been best friends since we were little kids. If you are here looking for him, he is not here. Did my mom let you in my house and into my room?" Kayla replies.

"Yes, Kayla, she did. She thought Ian might be back here with you. But since he is not here, when I'll make sure to tell your mom that it's just you back here. I'm sorry to have disturbed you, but I have to ask while I'm here, what are your plans for the day?" Brayden wants to get as much information from Kayla, to determine her actual state of mind or lack thereof.

"I think my mom and I have plans to go shopping. It will be the two of us, a 'girls' day out' she calls it. I can't wait and am so excited to spend the entire day with her. We are going to have so much fun having our day out. I really can't wait to see where she takes me this time. The last time we had our girls' day out, my mother took me into the big city of New York. It was so nice to get out of Brooklyn, even for a day. You know what I mean, right, Brayden? It is Brayden isn't it? Your name that is?" Kayla finishes.

"Are you being serious right now? You really don't know me or anything about what has been happening the past few months?"

"Yes, of course, I know what has been going on the past few months. My best friend Ian will be home soon, and we will give him the best surprise birthday party he has ever had. I can't wait to see him. Are you going to make it to his party tonight? It is going to be at his apartment. His mother and I did all the decorations. It is sure to be a blast. Well, I have to go too, Brayden, is it? My mom is expecting me, and I need to finish getting ready. You don't mind if I ask you to leave while I get ready for my day with my mother, do you?"

"No, I am okay with that. What else would a gentleman do? I'll make sure your mother knows that it is just you back here in your room alone. If anyone else comes looking for Ian, she will know not to interrupt you while you are getting ready for your 'girls' day out.'"

"That would be amazing if you would do that for me. I'm ready to get today over so I can go to Ian's surprise party tonight. He is his mother's 'special boy' as she puts it. I still don't know what she means by that. But to me, he is special, being my best friend. Wouldn't you agree, Brayden?"

"Why, yes, Kayla, that does sound awesome and like it is going to be an amazing time at Ian's surprise party. It's going to be held at his apartment, if I'm not mistaken, where you and his mother decorated," Brayden responds to Kayla's delusions as she stands up from her bed in her bedroom she created in her mind.

"Don't be late tonight for Ian's party," Kayla tells Brayden as he begins to exit her mind and return to where Connor is waiting.

Chapter 11

Searching?

"We are running short on time looking for Brayden and Connor together. We must search this entire compound, and together it's going to take us twice as long to complete the search. Do you think that maybe we could miss them if we are both searching for the same areas at the same time?" Garrett asks Maclaine.

As Garrett and Maclaine stop on the first floor and the elevator door opens, they both exit. Garrett allows Maclaine to exit first, of course. Garrett does not want to start any more trouble as he did just by pressing the elevator button for them to go down to the basement earlier. Now that they found out that Connor and Brayden have escaped their cells and are on the run, Garrett and Maclaine need to hurry.

"Are you sure we should check Kayla's room and the one next to hers before we check the rest of the compound? Do you really think that one of those two places are where they will go first, knowing they could find a way out of here if they looked hard enough? I mean, don't you at least think they will want to try to escape or try and contact Ian or the others to let them know where they are?" Garrett asks Maclaine.

"But you just agreed with me that those should be the first two places we should look. What's changed your mind in five minutes?"

"It hit me that Connor is the youngest, and he has, I bet, never been away from his sister Kenzie exceedingly long before, especially as a kidnapped child. I am sure he is just as worried about her as she is about him. Even though he knows we are here to protect them, he is still a child with childish instincts that may be getting to Kenzie as quickly as possible to make him want to flee. Now, this is just a suggestion, but we are closer to at least a few of the exits, which are much closer than either Kayla or the other room right now," Garrett gives an alternate suggestion to Maclaine for Brayden and Connor to suddenly want to escape.

"That does also sound like a plausible reason. Now we have a choice to make don't we? So, what do you think we should do first? I'm going to follow your lead on this one," Maclaine tells Garrett.

Garrett takes a few minutes to think about both options. He knows it is a ridiculously hard choice to make. Both are great ideas for how to search for Brayden and Connor.

"We need to check the exits first. If they are in either of those rooms and if they did not break out of here, they should still be in Kayla's room or the room next to hers when we get to them. So, if we think that is where they will end up, then what will it hurt by checking all the exits? If they are going to Kayla's room or the one next to it, they will still be there when we get finished checking all the exits and windows for breaches. Don't you agree?" Garrett explains how he feels about their situation to Maclaine.

"Okay, that does make sense. If we split up, we will be able to cover twice as much ground in half the time to see if they have left the compound before we need to check Kayla's room or the room next to hers. If, while we are searching the compound, we notice that an exit or window has been broken or tampered with, then we can assume that they have gone for the escape choice. But if there are no disruptions in the structure of the building's integrity, we can assume they are still in the compound in the last place we would look for them. So, if that is what we are thinking, don't you think it would be best to search the last place we would look **first**?" Maclaine challenges Garrett.

"Well, what do you think we should do then? Do you think we should split up or go together, or go straight to Kayla's room and possibly ruin things? You know there are more than likely cameras on her room door, and I would not be surprised if Mason has cameras in her room. Keep in mind that once we check the exits and windows, we would have to check all the other rooms together. Again, a waste of time. Then once we make sure those are all secure, together, they could have enough time to do whatever it is they have escaped to do, if it is not to leave the compound. It would be so much faster if we split up. With Connor's gift, we would be able to tell if they have left out any exit or window. Remember, Connor can move things with his mind, so there will be evidence they were there. Do you agree?"

"That does seem like an effective plan. We would make sure we do not waste time looking in rooms if they have already left the building or surrounding areas. If we were to search the compound rooms first, we could lose hours on where they could be, if they have already left here. I am not one hundred percent sure where this compound is or how long it takes to get to the school. Do you?"

"I don't even know what town we are in. Since I have never left here, I have no clue where Houston, much less the school, is from here or how long it would take to get there. Shouldn't that be your department, or have you never left here either?" Garrett clarifies to Maclaine, feeling a bit bad about the last statement he just made. Garrett does not know Maclaine well enough to make assumptions of how long he has been at the compound, nor what his circumstances are for being here in the first place.

"What I am responsible for here is none of your concern. All you need to know is that we are with each other and with Maria. I have been assigned to the same assignment you are, and that is to make sure Brayden, Connor, and Kayla get out of here safely. And somehow get you and me out with them as well. Not to mention this all needs to be done without being caught. Now, what do you say we get started searching and checking the exits for Brayden and Connor's escape? That way, we can get to search the interior, starting with the room next to Kayla's and then even hers, sooner."

"Fine, why don't you go that way, and I'll go this way. We can check each point of exit, including windows. Then once we are finished, we will meet back here. How do you feel about that?"

"And why exactly shall we go the way you are choosing? Is there something you are not telling me?"

"Yes, I am saying that this is the way you came from, and that way is the way I came from earlier. If we switch it up and I check your path, and you check mine, maybe one of us may see something the other did not notice on our way here. It is only common sense, wouldn't you agree? The more eyes on an area, the better, I always say."

"Yes, everyone knows what you are talking about. You do not have to explain yourself to me about everything you suggest. I am still wondering why you do that. So, why do you feel the need to over-explain everything to me all the time?"

"I'm not sure. It is something that I picked up at school from another student in my class that has Autism Spectrum Disorder. He would say something, then explain it in detail, even though everyone already knew what it was that he was speaking of. I kind of enjoyed the way he would detail things because just because I thought I knew something, he would explain that something with so much detail I would learn more from him than from the teachers. So, I have figured having more information is better than not having enough. Also, he taught me that every day was a day to learn something new. Sorry if it bothers you, but these are the times when you seem to need more information than you already have. Unlike popular belief, just because you think you know everything does not mean that you do," Garrett explains his reasoning for explaining things in such detail.

"I'm sorry if I offended you. I had no intention to do so. One of my closest friends also has ASD. So, I am familiar with it. Again, I am sorry. I was curious why you did it, but now I understand. My friend would also do things others thought were strange, but I began to pick up on some of them, and I still do them today."

"So, what are the patterns that you gained from your friend from school?"

"That is something we can talk about later. Right now, we need to get back to checking the exits and windows for our escapees, am I right?" Maclaine finishes.

"Yes, I would love to talk to you about what traits you have behaviorally picked up as I have. But for now, let us spit up and check our points.

***

As Garrett turns away from Maclaine, he is happy to learn of Maclaine's friend, who also has ASD. It is comforting to him to see that they may have more in common than he expected. But right now, he has a job to do. He must look for possible ways to escape the compound from where Maclaine came from, not sure what to expect. Garrett has only wondered around his side of the compound. So, this side will be a completely new adventure for him.

Garrett continues past the elevators for the first time he has been at the compound. To him, everything looks pretty much the same. That is until he reaches the control room. From the viewing windows, he sees the guards, the same guards Maclaine noticed as he passed them earlier, still asleep in the control booth. Garrett decides to take advantage of this moment and look at the security monitors. He is hoping to see Brayden and Connor in one of them.

The security monitors show just about the entire compound. Garrett begins with the cameras aimed at Kayla's bedroom and even the door to the room next to hers. Both monitors are clear of either Brayden or Connor. Garrett turns his attention to the exits that are on the side of the compound he has assumed responsibility for searching. From what he can tell, none of the exits or windows within any frame of a monitor down his side have been breached. But he knows he has to walk the area and check them out for himself.

Garrett turns his attention away from the security monitors and sleeping guards and continues his search down his assigned corridor, the one in which Maclaine's sleeping quarters are. *I wonder which room door is his. I am sure it is much nicer than my living arrangements here*, Garrett thinks to himself. *Well, I do not see anything that looks odd like a breakout has occurred. So, I think I will go ahead and start my way back to the elevators and wait for Maclaine.*

***

Now that Maclaine has been left alone by Garrett leaving him, he is relieved that he will be able to walk his assigned hallways without being bothered by Garrett. He has never been down these halls before. But then again, he has never had a reason to do so until now. Maclaine has stayed on his side of the hallway from the elevator, except when he was called to the room next to Kayla's by

Mason. He never really wondered what was on the other side of the elevators. Now that he has not only a reason to check out the other side of the compound, even if it is for escapees, but it is also still exciting for him. As he begins his adventure down his first hallway, he is reminded of the first time he met Maria.

***

Maclaine was walking down the hallway, and there she was, Maria, walking up to him in such an angelic way. He knew he could trust her from that moment on, so he spoke to her.

"Excuse me, Miss, are you in the correct area? I can tell you are looking around for something or someone. Can I help you?" Maclaine remembers asking Maria.

"Yes, I know exactly where I am. And what business is it of yours what I am doing here in the first place?" Maria snaps back to the guard in front of her.

"Sorry, my name is Maclaine. I am the security guard on duty tonight, and I am to report anything out of the ordinary to the lead guard," Maclaine answers back.

"So, what you are telling me is I am out of the ordinary for YOU, so you have to call this in? I am here to see Mason, and he is expecting me to be on time. Do you know if he is in his room or in the Control room that is just down the hall here?" Maria inquiries from Maclaine.

"Well, yes and no, if you must know the truth. But I mean no disrespect by the terms I have used. It is that we are under strict orders by Mason himself, to report anything, or anyone we have never seen here or met ourselves. Being that I have never seen you before, nor have we ever met, I must follow protocol and call you in here. Once they confirm you are who you say you are and what your reasons for being here are, I will allow you on your way. It should not take but a minute. Surely you have one minute you can spare to stay here with me, don't you?" Maclaine does his best to sweet talk Maria.

Once Maclaine finishes, Maria answers with a blush upon her cheeks. She is hoping he does not notice her cheeks. "Well, I guess I can spare a minute or two for you to check me out, with security, that is," Maria replies, tilting her head down, ever so shyly.

"Thank you, Ma'am. Give me just a moment now to confirm who you are and that you are scheduled to be here for a meeting with Mason. I'll be right over here," Maclaine tells Maria, as he is walking only a foot or two away from her to speak to the lead security guard on duty tonight.

As Maclaine moves away from Maria, she releases the fake smile she has been laying on him. She knows that she is going to need someone to help her from the inside of the compound. She uses her quick wit and interrupts Maclaine's call to security. She believes he will be perfect for her purpose. "Excuse me, Maclaine, is it? I hate to interrupt your call to clear who I am, but I've just noticed the time. If I am late, you know how Mason is, I may not get to see him at all tonight. And I drove all this way from Houston for this meeting. If I miss this meeting, I do not know when I will be able to get another, and this is very important. Is there any way you can skip the formalities? Just this once? For me?" Maria askes Maclaine with the application of her fake smile and blushed cheeks. This time she adds a little flutter of her long, beautiful eyelashes as she asks.

Maclaine knows then that she indeed knows Mason very well because of how she describes how he talks about being on time. It is the exact way to describe Mason. Maclaine gives Maria's smile, blushed cheeks, and fluttering eyes one last look and says, "If it were not for the way you described how Mason is with time, I would be saying 'No'. But the accuracy of your interpretation of how Mason will react if you are late is so spot on. I will say 'Yes' this one time. You can go ahead and make your way to your destination, which will be the Control room. That is where Mason is at the time. Would you like an escort, or do you know your way around already?"

Even though Maria knows she needs someone on the inside of Mason's compound, she knows she cannot move too fast with Maclaine. She needs to build up trust yet at the same time slip in bits and pieces of who Mason really is to get Maclaine to follow her more than Mason. "No, thank you, Maclaine. I know where the Control room is from here. I think I can find my way. I do hope to see you again when I come for another meeting with Mason."

"Do you have to wait for another meeting with Mason to come out to the compound? Can't you come back without a reason?" Maclaine shyly asks Maria.

Maria knows she can come back at any time, but she does not want to let Maclaine know that.

She wants to build that trust by lying to him, or more to his youthful instincts. "No, I come here by Mason's invitation, or unless I have something to tell him. Like a student at the Texas Academy of Arts. There could be one that comes along that he may be interested in. But I am sure you don't know much about the children, or as I call them, students, have to do with any of this, do you?" Maria asks Maclaine, sneaking in her first sign of trust in him.

"Are you speaking of why you are here tonight, or just in general?" Maclaine replies to Maria. "And what children?"

"Let us say, just in general. I am sure if you knew what I know, you would change your views on Mason. Sorry that I must leave you now, but you know about Mason's tardiness," Maria leaves Maclaine with those words to think about. As she scoots past him, "And please forget what I said about your views about Mason. I do not want to be on his bad side. Trust me when I say that."

"You have nothing to worry about. I will never repeat a word of what we did, or did not, speak of tonight. Except that you were given the all-clear by security, if I am ever asked, that is. Now you best be on your way to the Control room, every second counts right now," Maclaine assures Maria as she moves down the hallway with her head tilted back towards him. As if she is sizing him up to be a spy for her and her reason for being there. To Maclaine, it seemed more of just a "Thank you" from Maria, or a possible see you later. Maclaine is fine with either of the two. If he can stay on Mason and her good sides.

That is about the time Maclaine snaps back into reality. Once he is in real life, he has no clue where he is.

***

Maclaine was paying no attention to his surroundings as he continued his walk down the hallway, the same side of the compound as Garrett's room. That is after he wakes up from thinking of Maria. He has been walking around with his eyes closed, one could say.

"Where in the hell am I? Why have I not been this way before now? What are these chairs and couches doing here in the wide open, right in front of this entire glass entrance? What is this place we are living in?" Maclaine has more questions than answers at this point in his search for Brandon and Connor. He is beginning to understand what Maria was hinting at when he first met her, about Mason. The things about him that would change my views in him, which she never spoke of again. "Why did Maria stop talking about the truth about Mason? What is it she is trying to save me from?" That is the last of Maclaine's memories of Maria and his first meet, and the first time he had seen the main entrance of the compound that he had been living in. When he was brought here to join Mason's cause, he was brought in the back entrance.

"I think it would be best if I head back and meet up with Garrett. I do not want to be gone long or too much longer than he is at our meeting place. That could make me look suspicious, and I cannot afford any more unnecessary questions from Garrett," Maclaine says out loud, on his way back to the elevators, while hoping he makes it back before Garett does.

Chapter 12

Brayden Fills Kayla In?

"So, you are going to teleport us to Mason's compound? How do you know you can even teleport with another person or people for that matter?" Ian asks Kenzie in a skeptical voice.

"If you are asking if I have tried to teleport someone with me, the answer would be 'No.' I do have a good feeling about this though," Kenzie replies to Ian.

"What do you say we practice your teleporting first with either Jax or me, here at the school? At least before trying it at Mason's compound," Ian asks of Kenzie.

"I agree with Ian here, Kenzie. I think you may want to practice first here at the school before you try to teleport all of us to storm Mason's compound. I would feel more at ease knowing you have done it a few times before. You understand what I am trying to say here?" Jax is also pleading with Kenzie.

"Fine, I will practice my teleporting here, at the school with you two. Do you both feel better now?" Kenzie reveals a sense of defeat to Jax and Ian's request.

"Don't be upset, Kenzie. You know as well as we do that we can't always control our gifts, or they don't always go the way we want them to go. We have time for both of us to practice our gifts. I will admit I could use a little practice myself," Ian adds to his previous statement to Kenzie.

While Ian's statement does not completely change how Kenzie feels about the original statement Ian made, it does, however, lower her guard, knowing Ian needs practice as well.

Kenzie agrees to have a bit more practice trying to teleport with herself, then with an object, then with a person, before the actual mission.

"Perfect, we can begin tomorrow if that's okay with you?" Ian asks Kenzie.

"You want to practice with me?"

"Well, you will need at least one other person to practice with you if you want to try to teleport more than just yourself," Ian replies.

"Aren't you scared that I may mess up? What if I do something wrong and something happens to you? I don't think I'm ready for that just yet."

"Well, now you see the importance of training, don't you?"

"Yes, I do now. I can't let my emotions about saving Connor overpower my actual ability to judge a situation to achieve our goal. I'm sorry for being so snippy with you both earlier. I can tell I need patients, not only practice," Kenzie admins to the team.

"I understand what you are feeling. I sometimes let my feelings for saving Kayla overpower my own judgment," Ian admits.

Ian and Kenzie share a look of agreement, then both of them turn to look at Jax for instruction. They are both in shock to see Jax is almost crying.

"What's wrong, Jax?" Kenzie asks.

"It's just that that was so beautiful. Finally, seeing the two of you beginning to understand what being part of a team is really about," Jax replies.

"And what is that, may I ask?" Kenzie says back to Jax.

"They say that a true team works best when they realize they are more like a family. Which is what I believe you two have just figured out, and became family," Jax exudes excitement.

"Okay, Jax, we get your point. We should have been treating each other and acting like a family a long time ago. I can assure you that we will be a more effective team from this point on," Ian tells Jax with gratitude.

"Now that we have settled this family matter, can we not get started on my practicing?" Kenzie asks with a smile.

"What do you both say about us leaving Maria's room now and heading down to the training room, here at the school?" Jax asks Kenzie and Ian, with no complaints.

"Now, that sounds like a solid plan. I'm ready to leave Maria's room. You would think, by the way she acts, she would have a better taste in furniture. Or at least add some color to the room. This all grey and black color scheme is so depressing," Kenzie announces.

"I'm sure her room is just an extension of the person she is having to play, for Mason. I don't think Mason would truly trust someone with rainbows and flowers all over her clothes and home décor. Don't you agree?" Jax replies to Kenzie.

"I'm sure you are correct. Mason does not seem like someone who would trust anyone who is not wearing funeral clothes. I do hope you are reading Maria correctly and that she may have an actual personality under those clothes, home décor, and personal attitude!" Kenzie declares to Jax.

"I have known Maria for many years, and this is nothing more than a show for Mason. From what I remember about Maria, before taking over your mother's mission, she was nothing like this person now. Maria has always been a free-spirited soul, so her love for color is always shown through her love of painting" Jax clarifies.

"I have not stopped to put much thought into the sacrifices Maria must have had to make to take over for my mother. Her role is to infiltrate Mason's group and become part of his team to find out how to keep him from completing his mission. Guess my mother didn't know just how much she would be losing by not doing this job for the Believers. Does that mean Maria didn't have anything to lose?" Kenzie asks Jax in return.

"I wouldn't say Maria had nothing to lose because she lost almost as much as you did, in a way. But right now is not the time or place to discuss this right now. You and Ian should start your rigorous training. You both have a long way to go and a short amount of time to learn your powers. Even the one between the two of you, as Maria suggested. Now go, I will meet up with you both in just a bit. I need to clear up a few things with the head of the school before I meet you there. So run along!" Jax orders Kenzie and Ian.

With Jax's orders, Kenzie and Ian leave Maria's room to make their way to the training rooms in the basement of the school.

***

"Brayden! Wait! Don't leave me yet," Kayla explains out of nowhere.

"What's the matter with you, Kayla? I will be back in time for the surprise party you have planned for Ian. I know you and his mother worked very hard at this party, so I would not miss it for the world," Brayden replies, even out loud for Connor to hear.

What in the world could Kenzie and Brayden be talking about? Connor thinks to himself, feeling a bit confused. He is confused because of the one-sided conversation he is able to hear from Brayden, while Brayden is in Kayla's mind speaking to her.

"There is no party tonight," Kayla reveals with a boasting laugh.

"What do you mean there is no party tonight? What about all the planning you and Ian's mother have been doing?"

"So, you actually believed everything I told you?"

"Of course I did. I would never think you would make something up like that. Ian's your best friend, and what is so funny?"

"So you would say I will be able to fool Mason as well? Remember, you told me I had to be believable. Now, with you as the dream walker, and I convinced you of all of this charade, do you now think I can pass Mason's test?" Kayla comes clean with Brayden.

"NOW, I have to say that was some performance you put on. I am no longer worried about your skills of lying to Mason."

"Good, now when you came in, you asked me to take a seat. I guess you have something new to tell me since this is an unscheduled meeting," Kayla reminds Brayden.

"Like you can start with what Maria has done to me to make sure I stay asleep until she returns, along with who did she catch in her trap this time? That evil witch!"

"Well, there is something more about Maria that you don't know but need to know."

"I am pretty sure I understand just what type of a Mason follower she is. I know she is someone that cannot be trusted. She is neck-deep in all of this and she needs to be stopped along with Mason!" Kayla exclaims in anger.

"You see, that's just it. Maria is actually here to help us save you and destroy Mason. She has been planted..."

"There is no way that this woman is looking out for our best interest. She is a very cold person who only cares about herself. I have seen some of the things she has done, and none of them were in our favor," Kayla stops Brayden short.

"That's just it. Maria has been a double agent for the Believers. She was forced to take over the role after Mason did away with Kenzie and Connor's parents. Maria wasn't the first to be recruited by the Believers to infiltrate Mason's group and gain his trust in hopes of stopping him. But since the first recruit thought about leaving her children behind, she could not go through with the plan. So when Mason approached her about a deal, she declined.

Mason then followed the first offered recruit, Kenzie's real mother, home and erased her parents' memories. Mason then stole Kenzie and Connor and gave them to another couple to raise as their own, until he didn't need them anymore. But by that time, Kenzie and Connor had already escaped. Since Kenzie's mother could not breach Mason's group, they had to send someone else in, and that was Maria. This was the only way to keep Mason from finding the 'Time Keeper.' Everything was going as planned until the 'Time Keeper' showed up in Ian's possession.

"All of Mason's leads had dried up, then Ian's parents bought the 'Time Keeper' for Ian's seventeenth birthday. Once Ian had the 'Time Keeper,' everything started changing. Not just in his life, but in history as well. Then the ring you gave Ian for his eighteenth birthday combined with the 'Time Keeper's powers, is when you were erased from history. Ian was the only person who knew you were real and alive. He has never given up on finding you to bring you back to our timeline. That is the reason that Maria pretended to catch all of us. She did that to bring us back here to be closer to you and the compound to make sure we were already here when your rescue begins. I believe Maria kept you asleep until her return to make sure Mason couldn't speak to you, but I could. I am sure she is meeting with Jax, Ian, and Kenzie now to work on an escape plan on how to get you out of here and back in our timeline so things would be like they were before you were erased," Brayden fills Kayla in.

"Remember, I also told you that there was some stuff you would not believe or would have a hard time accepting what I'm telling you. This was a very risky mission for Connor and me, but we had no choice but to fill you in. Garrett and Maclaine are also our allies. We all just have to figure out, once we save you, how to bring you back from being erased."

"Now, there seems to be a ton of 'what ifs' lurking around this plan. What if Maria is paying you all? What do you all know about her? What does she have to gain, either by saving me or betraying us all and captures us all for Mason? Have. Any of you even thought of the motives she may have all of her own?" Kayla is trying to shed some other light on Maria.

"Well, we do know she never wanted this mission but was forced into it by the Believers. I'm sure she is ready to leave this dark world and the person she has had to become and go back to her previous life. Who would want to stay in this messed up world that Mason has created?" Brayden asks Kayla.

"I just don't want to put all my rescue efforts in the hands of one of the people that have placed us here, to begin with. We need to make sure Kenzie, Ian, and Jax have a backup plan, just in case."

"I hear what you are saying, and I believe Connor, myself, Garrett, and Maclaine are the backup plan. There are things we all can do that Mason has no clue about, and neither does Maria. I'm sure everything will go as smoothly as expected, so I need you to be ready when Maria wakes you up. If it is just the two of you, ask her questions, and see how you feel about her answers. Trust your gut about it.

Now I think it is time for Connor and me to leave you here and return to our cells before anyone notices we are gone. Don't you agree?"

"Yes, you are correct, and don't worry about me. I will be ready when Maria wakes me. Trust me," Kayla promises.

Brayden and Kayla share a smile, and Brayden releases his connection with Kayla and disappears from her mind and back into his own body, laying on the bed in the room next to Kayla's.

"Okay, Kayla is ready for whatever comes up next. How have things been out here?" Brayden asks Connor.

"So far, the coast has been clear, and no. alarms have gone off. We should be able to make it back to the cells before being caught," Connor proudly fills Brayden in on their current situation in the real world.

"Then what do you say? Are you ready to make a break for it?" Brayden asks Connor.

"You bet I am. Let me take another look to see if the coast is still clear."

Connor stands in front of the bedroom door, stepping on his tiptoes to look through the peephole, then he suddenly freezes.

"What's the matter, Connor? Why are you just standing there?"

"We are too late to make our great, unseen escape from here as we planned. I can see Garrett and Maclaine walking this hall now, checking the doors to all of the rooms," Connor expresses with a hint of fear in his voice. Then he sinks down and sits at the foot of the door, on the ground, and just looks up at Brayden with sadness on his face.

***

Maclaine heads back to meet with Garrett at the elevators that lead down to the empty prison cells of Connor and Brayden. He walks at a faster speed than usual, but not too fast to draw attention in case anyone is watching. Maclaine hopes he beats Garrett there or does not make Garrett wait long.

Maclaine makes his way around the corner to the front of the elevators, and there stands Garrett.

"What took you so long?" Garrett asks Maclaine.

"You should know that was an area that I have not been to before, so for me to examine and check for breaches was a bit taxing on me. You, at least, had an easy area to search. Did you find any possible? Escape routes the boys could have taken, you remember Connor and Brayden do you?" Maclaine is trying to turn things around on Garrett and off of himself.

"Cool your jets, Maclaine. No, I found no evidence of either of them escaping the compound. Did you find anything of interest?" Garrett asks Maclaine.

"Sorry, just seeing an entrance area I know nothing about left questions running through my mind. I didn't mean to shout at you, and no, I found no signs of escape. That means that they are still here, in the compound. How do you suggest we handle the room by room sweep?"

"Thank you for your apology and support. I say we go together and search each room from the elevators to Kayla's room. I have a feeling that they did not go far from Kayla. Now that they have been brought here, there is no way they are going to try and lose their advantage of being here in the compound during the rescue attempt," Garrett informs Maclaine.

"Now, that sounds like a solid plan. Also, if they see us coming, they will be less likely to make a run for it," Maclaine adds.

"You may be right about that, but Connor can throw us both out of his way if he is backed into a corner. We need to make sure they both know we are only looking for them, to help them get back to the cells before we are all busted," Garrett warns Maclaine.

"Good call. I love letting you take the lead on this one. You seem to have a way with people. So why don't we just start here?" Maclaine also shows he is afraid of what Connor can do.

The two of them begin checking each room door, locked, or unlocked. They went into the rooms to make sure they were empty or occupied by someone other than Connor or Brayden. They continued until they were just a few doors away from where Connor and Brayden were hiding.

"Let's keep searching. These are only a few more doors left anyway," Maclaine expressed to Garrett.

So they continued their search.

Chapter 13

Not Speeding?

Maria has been driving slower than her regular speed trying to avoid getting another speeding ticket. She knows she needs to get back to Mason's compound as quickly as possible, and she is not going to risk getting another speeding ticket. Maria figures, 'they have waited this long, so what's a little longer.'

As Maria pulls into the drive of Mason's compound, she notes that without speeding and getting pulled over by the police to receive a ticket, it is almost fifteen minutes longer to travel from Houston to the compound. *I could have avoided so many tickets and saved a ton of money by just driving the speed limit,* Maria thinks to herself.

Maria parks her car out of the way of the cameras. There is something she wants to try once she enters the compound before she meets with Mason. She is very aware that once he knows she is back, he will want to start right back up where they left off with Kayla. Maria needs to have a little time first to catch up with Garrett, Maclaine, Brayden, and Connor. She wants to inform them of why she left and why she is coming back empty-handed.

Maria gathers her belongings, opens her car door, and steps out. As she begins her exit from her car, her high heel shoe slips on a rock, causing her to drop her purse and other personal items. With her quick reflexes and now empty hands, she is able to brace herself with one hand on the car door and the other by grabbing the steering wheel. Unfortunately, the heel of her shoe did not survive the accident. Now she is not only trying to sneak into the compound, but she will be doing so with no shoes on and her hair looking disheveled.

"I sure hope there is no one out and about this late in the evening," Maria speaks to her embarrassed self as she walks up to the front doors. As she reaches the empty door's entrance, she takes a quick sneak peek into the front room to make sure it's clear as well. Feeling lucky that there is no one in sight, she swings the door open and makes it straight to the hall on the left side which leads to Kayla's room.

As Maria is rounding the corner, looking behind her to be sure no one is following her, she swears she faintly hears a door close. With that possibility, she stops and leans against the hall wall. Maria waits for just a few seconds, and after not seeing or hearing anyone, she takes off down the hall again. This time she makes it to Kayla's room. Maria pauses for a minute, then turns the doorknob slowly while pushing the door open. Maria now has to make sure no one is in the room with Kayla.

Once the door is open enough for Maria to stick her head in and take a good look around, she is able to verify that Kayla is alone in her room and still asleep on her bed. Maria quickly slides into the room, closes the door behind her, and locks it. Turning her attention back towards Kayla, who is lying on her bed asleep, Maria begins to make her way over to her. Once she reaches Kayla's bed, she places her personal items on the floor, softly. Maria looks at Kayla sleeping one last time, then snaps her fingers for Kayla to wake up. But nothing happens. Maria begins to panic now.

"Did I leave her under for too long? Did something go wrong? Or could someone else have done something to her? I have to wake her up, or she will never understand!" Maria panics out loud to herself.

"Understand what, Maria?" Kayla replies as she turns over in her bed to look at Maria directly in the eyes.

"Kayla! You are awake! Are you feeling okay?" Maria asks Kayla with excitement and concern.

"Yes, I am awake, unless you have planted yourself in my dreams. I feel fine, by the way, but let's skip all of these pleasantries and get to the point of what you did to me."

"And what makes you think I had anything to do with you being asleep?"

"Wow, you have a short memory. When you were in your panic mode, you just said, 'Did I leave her under too long' and 'Did I do something wrong.' Do I need to continue repeating all of your self-doubting questions you were asking yourself?"

"Fine. Yes, it was I who put a sleeping spell on you so I could go back to the school for an emergency meeting. I put you to sleep so Mason would not keep trying to have Brayden dream-walk you while I wasn't present. Do you remember if Mason continued while you were asleep?"

"I can assure you that Mason didn't even try again. So what was your emergency meeting about anyway? What could be more important to you than helping Mason get in my head, for whatever reason he wants in?"

"What I am about to tell you is going to be hard for you to believe, but it is all going to be the truth. I don't have much time for questions, so I will need you to just listen. Can you do that for me? Please?"

"Yes, I'm getting pretty used to being spoken to, but not being able to speak back, so fire away."

"First, I am here to stop Mason and whatever his plans are. My meeting at the school was with Jax, Kenzie, and Ian..."

"Ian? You saw and spoke to Ian? Is he okay?" Kayla interrupts Maria.

"Yes, the same Ian you know and who has never given up on trying to get you back to his timeline. I had to meet with them to discuss the best way and time for them to teleport here to be with Brayden, Connor, Garrett, Maclaine, and myself, to break you out of here. To break you all out of here and to stop Mason from completing his plans. So far, the only drawback is we don't know how Mason plans to go back in time to change his family's history. Until we can get him to reveal that, we only have half a plan.

"Now, this is where you come in, Kayla. Mason trusts you but also believes you know so much more than you have led him to believe. Don't worry, it's understandable, just look at me.

"So, what we need is for Mason to believe that Brayden has been able to break through your mind barriers and is able to walk your dreams and memories. We need Mason to tell Brayden what to look for in your mind, so we can also know what he needs to complete his plan. Once we have that information, we will be able to execute a full, fool-proof plan. Now, are you in with us, or not? We are running out of time. We are cutting it close to the final hour," Maria comes completely clean with Kayla.

Now it's up to Kayla to trust Maria and also trust her gut.

***

As Garrett and Maclaine get closer to the room next to Kayla's, the one where Connor and Brayden are stuck, Garrett hears someone coming in the front entrance of the compound.

"Did you hear that?" Garrett asks Maclaine.

"No. What do you think you heard?"

"It sounded like someone just came into the main entrance doors. Who could be coming in this late?"

"Well, I don't want to find out, so let's slip into the room next to Kayla's. It was going to be our last stop anyway," Maclaine suggests.

"Not a bad idea, Maclaine. We can kill two birds with one stone. We can search the room and hide in it at the same time. Come on. We don't have much time to get out of sight."

***

"Connor, you need to get up off the floor, NOW! Garrett and Maclaine are headed to this room right now, and in a hurry," Brayden whispers to Connor.

"Do you think they know we are in here?"

"I don't think so. It looks like they are trying to avoid something or someone. Let's find a hiding place in here, quickly, and be very quiet. Got it?"

"Understood," Connor agrees.

"Then let's get to hiding," Brayden demands, as they both run and find their hiding spots.

***

"Come on now, open the door," Maclaine ushers Garrett.

"I'm trying, but it's locked. Come here and help with getting it open, but quietly," Garrett demands.

Maclaine joins Garrett at the bedroom door, and together they push it open, with a slight popping noise. With that in mind, they run into the room but shut the door just a little too hard.

"What are you thinking, shutting the door that hard? Now I'm sure whoever just came in the front entrance surely heard our door shut," Garrett scolds Maclaine while taking a glance through the door peephole.

"Sorry, we were in a rush. Anyway, now that's the past, so what do you see? Anything?" Maclaine asks.

"No, not yet, but give it a minute. Why don't you go sit down and quit stressing me out? I will keep an eye out for a few more minutes to make sure no one comes to this room," Garrett strongly suggested to Maclaine.

"Fine, I'm getting tired anyway. We might as well get prepared to take our punishment since we have lost Connor and Brayden."

"Well, you have sort of found us now," Brayden speaks from his hiding place under the bed.

"Wait a minute, who said that and where are you?" Maclaine asks in shock.

"It's me, Brayden. I'm under the bed, and Connor is here in this room as well. He is behind the chair you are sitting in."

About that time, Connor reaches over the back of the chair he has taken for his hiding place and taps Maclaine on his shoulder. That small tap sent him shooting out of his seat like a rocket into space, landing right next to Garrett, who was laughing at the situation.

"We will have to deal with you two later, but right now we believe someone is out in the hall. So you could please keep it quiet for a few more minutes," Garrett instructs Connor, Brayden, and even the scared Maclaine.

They all follow Garrett's orders and sit in silence. They will wait until Garrett gives them the 'coast is clear.' Little do they know that call is not going to be very long.

The next thing they notice is Garrett backing away from the door's peephole, with his finger over his lips, motioning for the others to remain quiet. The others follow his lead.

Garrett then makes his way over to the wall that connects the room they are in with Kayla's room and motions for the others to do the same. Once they are all in place, Garrett motions for everyone to press their ears against the wall, they all follow suit.

At first, they can hear the door open and close, but whoever is in the room with Kayla is unable to be heard clearly. All they hear are muffled sounds. They all look at Garrett with a 'what do we do now' look, but he is just standing there as if he can hear them just fine.

***

"Kayla don't be alarmed, but it's me, Garrett. I am only here to hear what she is doing here and if you have any questions after she has finished. I may be able to answer some of the questions, so act naturally to Maria, okay?" Garrett tells Kayla in her mind as he has entered her body again.

"Fine, but we are doing this my way. You will not interfere with the way I act or speak to Maria. Do you understand? These are my rules you must obey if you would like to continue using me," Kayla thinks back to Garrett.

"Agreed, now just pretend I am not even here."

"That should be easy!" Kayla thinks back to Garrett.

"Understand what, Maria?"

***

"Wow, you are getting very good at controlling your teleporting, Kenzie. Do you think you are strong enough to try it with another person yet?" Ian boasts about her progress.

"Thank you, but I want to hold off on trying a human trial run, for now. Right now, I have a feeling there is more I can do with the freezing part of my teleporting," Kenzie replies, taking her training very seriously.

"What do you mean? You feel that you may be able to control what you freeze, or for how long even?" Ian asks.

"To be honest, I'm not 100% sure what I feel. That's why I want to start focusing on this now. That may have something to do with both of our powers combined, to speed up time. Either way, I have to explore this gift. It was given to me for a reason, and I want to learn how to use it and not be scared of it."

"Well, you keep trying with your freezing powers, and I will try to see what I may be able to do to help speed up the timeline as well, combined with your freezing gift. I'm not even sure where to start. Could it be something to do with the 'Time Keeper' or my ability to create portals with a reflective surface?" Ian replies to Kenzie with uncertainty.

"Stop overthinking it, Ian. You need to stop letting your mind control your actions, just for a little bit, and let your heart and gut feeling lead you. If you feel something different, or even strange to you, just go with it. You may be surprised to find out what your body has been trying to tell you. Now, I'm going to let you find your inner voice while I go and listen to mine. Let's meet back up in an hour," Kenzie encourages Ian not to give up.

Ian agrees and turns to walk back over to his training area. As he walks away from Kenzie, he begins to try and listen to his heart and gut instead of his brain. Just as Ian is almost at his training station, the 'Time Keeper' begins to vibrate ever so softly. It is enough for Ian to feel, and he closes his eyes and tries to listen to what it is trying to tell him. Ian stops and tries to force his heart to open up and listen, but he is getting nothing. After a few minutes of trying, he gives up and opens his eyes, and continues to his station. Then "IT" happens.

Ian is suddenly stopped in his tracks, with visions shooting through his mind. The visions are of him and Kenzie, working together but not really showing him what they are supposed to be doing. The visions do not repeat and only begin to go faster as if time is speeding up. Then they stop, and Ian is released.

"Kenzie, did you just free me?" Ian yells over to her.

"How did you know it was me that did that?"

"Because, when you did, I had all of these flash visions of you and me speeding up time. How were you able to free me this time? Every other time you have teleported, I was the only person that never froze. I figured I was immune to your powers," Ian asks.

"I'm not sure. I just felt you feeling troubled, so I closed my eyes and focused on helping you see what you needed to see. It's hard to explain, but I guess it worked."

"I guess you could say it did, in a way, but I have no clue what the flash visions mean for us to do to actually pull this time speed off. Where in the world is Jax? When we need him, he's nowhere to be found," Ian asks out loud to anyone who may be listening.

"And what do you think Jax can do for us now? We are doing fine on our own, right now, do you agree?"

"Kenzie, I say we speed up your training, and you teleport both of us to where Jax is right now!" Ian is not requesting Kenzie.

"Are you serious, or have you completely lost your mind? First, I have no clue where Jax is for us to teleport to, and second, you want me to use you as my first human trial with my teleporting?"

"Yes. I believe if you think of Jax, like the way you enter his thoughts, you can find him, and I believe you can do this with me. We need to get to Jax, NOW. If you can think of a faster way, I'm all ears," Ian suggests.

"Okay, hold on to me while I try to find Jax's mind, then take a deep breath because I will not give any warning when I do find him, and we teleport. We will just go to him, at least I hope so. So are you sure you are ready for this," Kenzie wants to make sure Ian is actually aware of the risks they are taking and okay with them?

"Yes, so let's do this!"

"Here we go," Kenzie says as she shuts her eyes, then, next thing they know, they vanished.

Chapter 14

Breakout Foiled?

"Garrett, are you able to make out what is being said in Kayla's room?" Maclaine asks.

Even though Maclaine just asks him a question, Garrett makes no moves or any type of acknowledgment that he has even heard Maclaine. Garrett is just standing there with his ear still pressed to the adjoining wall to Kayla's room, with a blank look on his face.

Maclaine begins to wave his hand in front of Garrett's face, but even that does not affect Garrett. "What is wrong with you, Garrett? I need you to snap out of whatever this is, so we can get a move on while whoever is in Kayla's room is still there. Do you hear me?"

Garrett is still standing there with a glazed look in his eyes and no response.

Maclaine, now getting desperate, raises his hand back and gives Garrett a slight slap on the back of his head. To his surprise, that seems to have done the trick and brought Garrett back to attention.

Garrett begins to shake his head while rubbing the back of it. "Why did you hit me? We still have plenty of time to make it back to the cells with Connor and Brayden," Garrett tells Maclaine.

"And just how do you know this? Are you telling us that you can hear what is being said in there while none of us can hear anything?" Maclaine comments.

"Let's just say one of my gifts is the gift of listening. You should give it a try sometime. Now, may I get back to trying to listen in on what is being said in there?" Garrett snaps back at Maclaine.

"How about this? How about I go ahead and take Brayden and Connor back to their cells while you stay here and listen all you want? If you finish in time and want to meet us in the basement before I leave, you can fill us in then. I am starting to get tired from all of this running around, and I'm sure these guys are ready to get back to their amazing cells, right guys," Maclaine suggests to Garrett while at the same time asking Brayden and Connor.

"Yes, we would like to leave this room and go back to our cells now," Brayden tells Garrett and Maclaine.

"Fine, take them back to the basement. I will not be far behind you as I still want to speak to both of you to find out why you have risked so much for this outing of yours," Garrett tells the three of them.

Maclaine motions with a nod to Garrett as an understanding, then a nod to Connor and Brayden as instructions to follow him. Maclaine walks over to the door, but before he can grab the doorknob and twist it open, Connor has already cracked it open without a sound. Maclaine snaps a quick look back at Connor, who is just smiling, then he turns back to check the hallway through the cracked door.

Being that the coast is clear for the three of them to make their getaway, Maclaine leads the way out of the bedroom with Connor and Brayden in tow. As they make their way to the elevators, Connor motions to Maclaine the locations of the guards they had to knock out and hoped they were not awake yet. Maclaine takes note and speeds up their pace.

Taking them only a few minutes to make it to the elevators, they quickly pressed the call button when the door opened right up. With that sign, they all three jump into the elevator and press the basement button. The elevator doors close, and they all relax for a least a minute.

Stopping on the basement floor, the doors open, and they are all holding their breath, again still hoping for an empty room. To their recurring luck, the room is empty.

"Perfect, now the two of you need to get back in your cells and shut and lock the doors back," Maclaine says while looking at Connor. "You do understand what I am saying, don't you?"

"Yes, sir. I understand very well. You don't like anyone helping you out. You are like a one-man show and feel that a team just slows you down. But don't worry, soon you will see that with all of us working together, things will be much easier, faster, and efficient. You can count on that," Connor releases what he has been thinking about Maclaine since he first met him.

"Well, do you feel better now that you got that out of your system? It seems you have been holding that in for some time now. For your information, I have been working with Maria for a long time, and it has just been the two of us. Yes, you can say I like to work alone because that is what I have been used to doing. And you may be right, and I may see things differently about working with a team, so you let me know when one arrives because you two sure are not acting like you are part of any team but your own. Next time be careful about who you are trying to offend because it could be you that winds up offended. I think I will go ahead and leave you both here to wait on Garrett. I have had enough for one evening," Maclaine tells Connor and Brayden as he turns and steps back into the elevator, not saying another word.

"Why did you have to go and say all of that to Maclaine? You know he is trying to help us, don't you?" Brayden asks Connor.

"I felt it was something that needed to be said, and I suppose what he said about us is something we needed to hear as well. Don't you agree?" Connor accepts Brayden's remarks.

"True, he was pretty much right on point with the way we have been excluding them. Maybe that is something we should talk to Garrett about when he shows up," Brayden suggests to Connor.

They both return to their cells, with Connor shutting and locking their doors after they make it into their cells. They both sit in silence and wait for Garrett.

***

Once Garrett could tell that Maria is getting close to ending her conversation with Kayla, he goes ahead and excuses himself from Kayla's body. He then makes his escape from the room to the elevators, the elevators that lead down to the basement cells where Connor and Brayden should be by now.

Now that he is satisfied to see them both with his night-vision goggles, he walks over to them.

"So, who would like to start? Start by telling me what you were thinking, leaving this room, and risking getting caught?" Garrett demands answers.

Brayden begins to fill Garrett in on his and Connor's mission and why they chose to do it. They spoke for about twenty minutes, and Garrett just sits there in 'awe.'

"You both risked all of this to make sure Kayla was going to be okay?" Garrett clarifies.

"Well, yes. We did not know how long she would be asleep, and we didn't want her to go crazy," Brayden explains.

"So, how long have you been able to dream-walk Kayla or break through her mind barriers?"

"I actually broke through her barriers the last time I said I couldn't connect with her and explained a few things with her and why I was there. But this was the first time I was able to have a long conversation with her. It, of course, took longer than expected because she had to play a joke on me to prove she will be able to lie to Mason and myself when I do actually dream-walk her for Mason. I have to say it was a very good performance. I almost left because I believed her."

"If you fell for it, then it must have been a pretty amazing performance. I need to head off to my room and make sure we are all rested because tomorrow is the day Mason tries again with Kayla. Now, get some rest, and I will be back soon to get you," Garrett tells Connor and Brayden as he turns and makes his way to the elevator to head up to his room.

***

Maria finished filling Kayla in on her meeting with Jax, Ian, and Kenzie, along with her involvement with them to defeat Mason's plans. Now she has left Kayla to meet with Mason to let him know she is back. She knows that no matter how late it is, Mason will want to know of her arrival. Maria knows that he will more than likely be pacing in his office, unable to sleep until he can get back to work on getting into Kayla's mind.

Maria walks up to Mason's office door and gives it a swift knock. Mason must have been expecting her, even at this time of night, because his office door opens with such quickness.

"It's about time you made your way back. So, what do you have to show for your need to leave us during a most important breakthrough?" Mason scolds Maria.

"Well, it turns out that there was a small fire on the floor where my room is located. Luckily, my room was undamaged, but the smoke and fire alarms set off my own personal alarms. But everything is fine on my end, thank you for asking," Maria fires back at Mason.

"No need to be smart with me. I am in no mood. Your items can always be replaced. The time we have now lost, because of your absence, can't be replaced. With that being said, I think we should wake up the others, except Kayla, of course, and start back up where we left off," Mason insists.

"I'm sorry that I had to leave, but I am in no condition to do anything else tonight. Is there any way we can wait for just a few more hours? So I may get some rest and then freshen up. I know this is the last thing you want to hear right now, but to be honest, it would be for the best," Maria begs Mason.

Mason stands there, in front of Maria, not believing what he is hearing from her. Is Maria really asking me to put this off even longer? Mason thinks to himself. But before he has a chance to answer Maria out loud, Maria begins to speak.

"Mason, this really is not much of a request. You are going to need me rested up if you are going to want me to be able to keep Kayla asleep. If I weaken anymore, the spell I put on her could break, then you will have to wait for her to go back to sleep on her own. So the question really is, how much time are you willing to give up just for a little rest for me?"

"If you believe this is going to be for the best for what I am trying to accomplish, then fine. Why don't you go and take about five hours to rest and freshen up? But after that five hours, I don't want to hear any more excuses to cause us to postpone getting into Kayla's mind. Do you understand me?"

"Yes, you have made yourself perfectly clear. Thank you for the extra time. Now, if you don't mind, I want to make sure I use every minute of your generosity," Maria expresses to Mason as she turns and begins to walk down the hall towards her room.

***

As Ian and Kenzie are flying through what Ian can only describe as space, he tries to reach out to Junior.

Junior? Can you hear me? Ian thinks to himself.

Yes, I am here. What can I do for you? Junior replies.

I want to inform you that Kenzie and I will be ready tomorrow with the ability to speed up time to go and save Kayla and the others. I need you to please go and let the others know to be ready because we only have one shot at this mission. Can you do that for us?

Yes, I have someone there I can contact, but I am not sure they will be happy with a time limit.

Let them know they have had plenty of time, plus they will be getting two days of work done in just only one day. So they will still be able to do what they want to complete or try.

That sounds fair enough. I will tell my contact there so they can inform the others to make sure everyone is ready. Good luck tomorrow! Junior thinks back to Ian as he leaves his mind.

***

Maclaine is fast asleep when he first hears a knock on his bedroom door.

"Who is it?"

"It's me, Maria. I need you to get up and be ready in ten minutes. Mason is waiting on us to begin again with Kayla. Will you also give Garrett a call and give him the same instructions as you have just received? I will stop by and make sure Connor and Brayden are away and getting ready, so when Garrett is ready and on his way to meet us, stop by the cells and grab Connor and Brayden to bring with you. You know where we will be at, the room next to Kayla's," Maria directs Maclaine.

"You got it. We will see you and Mason in ten minutes," Maclaine confirms with Maria.

Maria leaves Maclaine's door, leaving him to get out of bed, call Garrett, and explain what Maria has instructed them to do. After Maclaine finishes with Garrett, he hangs up the phone and decides to skip even a quick shower. Maclaine rushes over to his dresser and picks out a clean outfit for today's events.

Once he has gotten dressed, he exits his room and heads towards the elevators. That is the meeting place he set up for him and Garrett.

Upon his arrival, Maclaine notices Garrett coming down the hall from his room. As Garrett strolls over to Maclaine, the elevator door has already opened. Maclaine pressed the call button when he first arrived and saw Garrett making his way to meet with him to get Connor and Brayden.

They both enter the elevator, neither with even a 'Good Morning,' as they are both still very tired from last night's events. They ride the elevator down to the basement, wait for the door to open, then they exit. They grab a pair of night vision goggles to check and see if Brayden and Connor are ready. To their surprise, they are both standing just in the shadows by the elevator.

"Don't worry, Maclaine. Maria opened the doors for us and asked that we wait here until you two showed up to pick us up. This way we save some time," Connor says to Maclaine in a more apologetic tone than the one he was using with him just a few hours ago.

"Thank you for letting us know, Connor. I appreciate your honesty and following her instructions," Maclaine replies with an apology. "If you both are ready for today, then let's get a move on so we are not late."

"We are ready," Braden answers.

"Then let's get a move on. After you two, if you don't mind?" Garrett expresses this to Connor and Brayden.

Maclaine and Garrett follow the other two into the elevator, pressing the button for their next floor. The ride up is just as quiet as the ride down, when it was just Maclaine and Garrett. It seems like none of them are early morning people.

The stop of the elevator and its opening door is their sign to make their exit. One by one, they exit the elevator with Maclaine in the lead and Garrett in the rear. This is all for show of course. They make their way to the door to the room next to Kayla's, and enter without even knocking.

"Well, it's about time you all decided to join us. I hope you are all ready for a hard, full day's work, because I know I am," Mason says just to be speaking.

"Since we are all here now, why don't we get started, Mason? I'm pretty tired, so getting to dream walk Kayla sounds awesome for me. By the way, you still have not even told me what you are wanting to find out, or what you are wanting me to look for in Kayla's mind," Brayden speaks with a hint of sarcasm.

"You are correct. I have not told you anything yet, because you have not been able to actually get into Kayla's mind. Break through her mind barriers and have yourself a dream walk, and then I will let you know what I am looking for," Mason requires of Brayden.

"Fine. Let me lay down so I can get to work, while you all just stand around and watch," Brayden snaps at everyone.

Brayden makes his way to the bed, takes his place on it, and closes his eyes. It does not take him long to connect to Kayla's mind. Since she has already permitted him to enter, she is there waiting for him.

"I'm in," Brayden says out loud. "How do you want me to prove it to you?"

"Have Kayla think about the one day we had off, just the two of us, and tell me what you see," Mason instructs Brayden.

Did you get all of that, Kayla? Think about your only day off with Mason. A day that was just for the two of you, Brayden thinks to Kayla, so the others don't hear him.

Okay. Here goes nothing, and I really mean nothing, Kayla thinks back to Brayden with a giggle.

Kayla begins to think of that day they were supposed to have off together, just her and Mason. But the one thing that sticks out the most is how relieved she was when Maria ended their day early by interrupting them for an important meeting with Mason, alone.

"Mason, she does not have any fond memories of that day to think of, except one. That is when Maria showed up and interrupted your day with Kayla for some secret meeting with you alone. So you let her go back to her room without escorts for the first time. How is that for proof?" Brayden asks.

Mason is not happy with the answer, but Maria can confirm that she did interrupt their day, and he let Kayla go on her own to her room.

Now, Connor, Maclaine, and Garrett all think it very funny and begin to snicker.

"That's enough. Yes, you have proven your point, now break your connection with Kayla, so we can discuss what I need from her," Mason instructed Brayden.

I'll be right back, Brayden thinks to Kayla, then wakes up for further instructions.

Chapter 15

Time and Teleporting?

"WOW! That was super strange. I didn't think I could actually do it," Kenzie boasted to Ian once they reappeared next to Jax from the training room.

"I have to agree with you, that was some trip. But I knew you could do it. Now, where exactly are we?" Ian asks Kenzie as they both are looking around.

"It looks like we are in the Headmaster's office, but who is the older lady in here with Jax and the Headmaster?" Kenzie asks.

"I think that is the Chancellor of the Believers, Billie June. I wonder what she is doing here. Can you unfreeze Jax so we can talk to him?" Ian says to Kenzie.

"Let me try," Kenzie replies.

Kenzie closes her eyes and thinks of Jax, and the next thing they know, Jax is aware of their presence and is very confused.

"What in the world are you two doing here, and how did you get here?" Jax is not happy about their intrusion.

"We are very sorry to interrupt your meeting, but we are on the verge of figuring out how to speed up time, and as you can see, we can already teleport together! Some things happened in the training room, and I saw some visions. But I can't make heads or tails of them, and that was only after Kenzie was able to freeze me in the training room. That is why I begged her to bring us to you, so you may be able to shed some light on what they mean. Oh, and I also may have told Junior that we would be there tomorrow because I know you can help us figure out the speed time power we should be able to do," Ian fills Jax in on pretty much everything.

"When did you have time to talk to Junior? You grabbed me, and we came straight here right then," Kenzie is asking Ian in shock.

"It's a long story, but that's not really our problem right now. Jax, we need you now to help us. Can you get out of this meeting quickly or what?" Ian desperately asks.

"This is way too much to process in just a few seconds. You will need to let me speak to the Headmaster and the Chancellor of the Believers, and then I can meet you back at the training rooms. Do you think you two can go back and practice some more for just a few short minutes, and I'll be right there?" Jax asks as politely as possible.

"Yes, I'm sure Kenzie can get us back in one piece, but you must not take your time. We have a ton of things to confirm and no time to do it all in," Ian replies.

"Are you sure you can do this, Kenzie? Or would you rather walk back to the training rooms?" Jax wants confirmation from Kenzie.

"Walk? Are you kidding me? I got this! If you are ready, grab hold of my hands, and we will see you in a few minutes, Jax. Don't make me come back for you myself," Kenzie replies while looking at Ian.

Ian grabs Kenzie's hands, and poof, they are gone again. Then just like they left the Headmaster's office, they are back in the training rooms.

"Now, when did you have time to contact Junior and tell him all of that?" Kenzie asks Ian.

"Well, this may be hard to believe, but while we were in transition from the training room to the Headmaster's office, I was able to reach out to Junior with my mind and explain things to him. I even asked him to inform the others we will be there in two days, but we will be there tomorrow for us. It was pretty awesome," Ian explains. "Now, I guess we can get back to practicing while we wait on Jax.

***

Garrett? Can you hear me? It's me, Junior. Ian sent me to speak to you, Junior thinks to Garrett's mind, because he knows he is the only person he can connect to while asleep or awake.

Garrett stops giggling at what Brayden has just said about Mason and Kayla's day off. *What are you doing contacting me during the day again and while I'm with Mason?* Garrett thinks back to Junior.

I told you that Ian sent me. He wants me to tell you that he and Kenzie have figured out how to speed up the time to two days, and they will be here tomorrow.

What do you mean tomorrow? We haven't even found out what Mason is looking for in Kayla's mind. That is a very bad idea.

Ian wants me to let you know that even though they will be here for what's tomorrow for them, it will be two days past for us. Ian is just speeding up time, not removing two days. So you will still be able to do all the things you will do in two days. But as I said, it will only be one day for them.

Well, I better inform the others of the upcoming plans in two days, for us, that is.

That's when Ian is expecting you to do.

Fine, I will let them know and just hope we are able to do everything we need to do before they come here tomorrow, for them, that is.

I do as well, so good luck, Junior thinks to Garrett before he leaves his mind.

***

"Okay, I need everyone to please step out into the hallway while I speak to Brayden alone," Mason requests of everyone in the room.

"You heard him, now step outside and wait until we call you back inside," Maria tells Connor, Garrett, and Maclaine.

"You must be confused, Maria. That also means you need to step outside along with the others until I call you all back in," Mason clears things up for Maria's confusion.

"Excuse me? You want to speak to Brayden, alone, without me?" Maria asks Mason with anger.

"That would be the meaning of the word 'alone,' now wouldn't it? So you heard me just fine. Do not make me repeat myself. Please make your exit with the others so Brayden and I can begin our conversation. Now shut the door behind you on your way out," Mason orders Maria.

Without another word, Maria turns around and makes her exit through the bedroom door, giving it a slightly harder slam than usual to close it. She continues to huff and puff the entire time she has to wait in the hallway with the others.

"Now that we have the room to ourselves, it's time you knew what it is that I am looking for in Kayla's mind. Now, once I tell you about these two things, you will not need to speak out loud anymore while you are connected with Kayla's mind. The others are not to know anything about what I am looking for. And if you value your friends' lives, you will keep what you find out between just you and me. Do you understand me?" Mason lays down his conditions of not following the rules he has just laid out for Brayden.

"Yes sir, I understand. I will only tell you what I find out," Brayden promises.

"Great, that's good to know. Now there are going to be two things you are going to find out for me. The first thing I need to know is how exactly Kayla knows a woman named Alexis. The second thing I need to know is about the silver ring of Ian's. I have a feeling she has seen it before and knows exactly where it came from. You got it? Just those two simple things," Mason finishes telling Brayden what he needs from Kayla's mind.

"Got it. Find out how she knows some lady named Alexis and see what she knows about Ian's silver ring. I can handle two jobs at one time," Brayden gloats to Mason.

"I guess we will see, because not only do your friends' lives depend on your work but also yours. That should be some incentive to make sure you do your job."

Brayden takes a deep breath and shakes his head, and lays down again on the bed.

Mason walks over to the door, opens it, and motions for the others to come back into the room. No one really cared about not getting to listen, except Maria, so she stormed in last.

"Please close the door softly this time, Maria. We are not trying to wake everyone up in the building," Mason tells Maria without even looking at her.

Maria slowly closes the door and moves over to take a seat in a chair with a view of Brayden on the bed.

"Okay, Brayden, remember what we discussed, and go ahead and connect with Kayla's mind again."

***

"Are you ready?" Jaxs asks Kenzie.

"Ready as I'll ever be. Now each of you take a hand," Kenzie orders Jax and Ian. "Take a deep breath and be prepared for anything. I am going to focus on Connor and try to take us to where he is in two days from now."

Jax and Ian take a deep breath, and the next thing they know, they are no longer in the school. By the time they can exhale, they are standing in a room with Mason, Maria, Connor, Garrett, Maclaine, and Brayden.

"How did you all get here?" Mason is shouting at the three intruders.

"Kenzie, why are they all not frozen?" Jax asks.

"I think it's because I teleported the three of us, and my powers did not work because of the extra usage of my teleporting. I just don't have enough energy to do both," Kenzie suggests as she stumbles a little light-headed.

"You teleported all three of you here? How fascinating. We have been working on the final pieces of what I need from Kayla, or should I call her Alexis, for the past two days. How long did it take you to get here?" Mason inquires.

"We just left the school now, but two days ago for you. We also sped up time to make sure you got what you needed from Kayla before we stopped you," Ian speaks out proudly.

"Guards, get in here NOW!" Mason begins to shout again.

As he commands, eight new guards come bursting through the bedroom door. Not only is this a surprise to Ian, Kenzie, and Jax, but also the others that have been using the room with Brayden and Mason for the past few days.

"Mason, what is the meaning of this? Why have you had extra guards outside the door this entire time?" Maria wants answers.

"Let's just say 'a little birdie' told me to be extra prepared for today and to be ready for anything. Do you think you are the only person in this room with secrets? As usual, I am one step ahead of you again," Mason unknowingly shows his cards about his foreign body visitor.

"Guards grab those three and take them down to the cells, along with these two," Mason says while pointing at Connor and Brayden.

The guards do as they are told, and grab the five total captors, and begin to escort them out of the room when Mason suddenly stops the two with Ian and Kenzie.

"These two will stay here, but the rest may go to the cells. Once they are all locked up, come back up here, and take your posts back at this door.

Now Kenzie, Ian, go ahead and take a seat. This will not take long," Mason finishes with all of his orders.

Ian and Kenzie move to sit in seats that are not near each other, but Mason catches on quickly and puts them side by side.

"Nice try, but it is obvious that your powers work together, so sitting next to each other only seems logical.

Now Brayden was not able to retrieve all the information from Kayla's mind, but what I have found out over the past two days, and that I have both of you and you can teleport people with you Kenzie and speed up time Ian, then you should be able to do the same, except go back in time. You two are what I have been searching for my entire life. You are going to take me back to the beginning of when my family broke down with yours, Ian. You are going to take us back to the time your great-family member Sebastian and my great-family member Grayson were friends, and we are going to force Sebastian to give his powers and control of the 'Time Keeper' to my family member, Grayson. Do you understand our quest?" Mason reveals his plans to the five of them, Maria, Garrett, Maclaine, Ian, and Kenzie.

"We are not even sure we can achieve something like that. And even if we could, what makes you think we would do it for you anyway?" Ian tells Mason.

"Oh, I'm sure you two can figure out very quickly how to make it happen, and even though you may think you don't have much to lose, Kenzie may think differently. Am I correct Kenzie?"

"Connor?" Kenzie says out loud.

"Yes, your brother. You sure would not want to see anything happen to him, would you? Then you will work with Ian and do as I ask and do this. If you do then no harm will come to you or your brother. No harm will come to any of you, you have my word," Mason promises.

"You have no clue what you can promise. Once you go back and change the past, all of the present and future is gone as we know it. It will become an entirely new future, one in which you may not even exist," Ian tells Mason.

"Well, that's just a chance we will have to take, now won't we? Now, whatever it was you did to teleport here, I need you to do it again, but just back in time with a memory from the 'Time Keeper.' And I know you have access to all of your previous family members that have stored it, including Sebastian's. Do it now, or I'll have Connor taken care of right now!"

"No, don't! Kenzie, do exactly what you did before, except instead of focusing on Connor, think of the memory in my head that I will be accessing through the 'Time Keeper.' Do you think you can do this?" Ian asks of Kenzie.

"I'm not sure, but it does sound logical. Now, both of you grab my hands, close your eyes, and take a deep breath. I'm not sure how long this trip will take to go back this many years," Kenzie instructs Mason and Ian.

They both do as Kenzie instructs, and as they take the deep breaths, they vanish from the room next to Kayla's.

Chapter 16

Visiting the Past?

Ian, Kenzie, and Mason reappear in an alley behind the bar where Sebastian and Grayson ended up fighting, causing Sebastian to lose the 'Time Keeper.' As soon as Ian and Mason let go of Kenzie's hands, she fell to the ground, exhausted.

"Kenzie, are you okay?" Ian asks worriedly about her condition as he kneels beside her.

"Don't worry about her right now, and tell me about where we are," Mason tells Ian.

"Mason, I will tell you about this location if you get over here and help me with Kenzie. Remember, if you are successful in having Sebastian transfer his power of the 'Time Keeper' to Grayson, Kenzie is the only one who will be able to take us back to the present. Or do you want to be stuck here in this time period forever and never know if your plan works?"

"You win, Ian," Mason responds as he makes his way over to kneel on the other side of Kenzie, to help Ian.

"Kenzie, can you hear me?" Ian asks while rubbing her arm.

"Yes, I can hear you," Kenzie replies in a very soft voice, still with her eyes closed.

"Great, you are fine. Ian, now you can tell me about this place."

"Hold your horses, Mason. Kenzie may have spoken, but she is not fine. Kenzie, what's happening to you? What do you need?" Ian asks.

"I need something to drink and to sit up and lean against something. I just need to rest for a few minutes. That trip took a lot out of me," Kenzie explains.

"Mason, can you go see if you can get a glass of water from inside that place right there?" Ian asks as he points at the door in the alley closest to them, "and come right back. The sooner we get Kenzie stronger, the sooner we can try to do what you came here to do."

"That door there?" Mason replies with a small smile. "Are you sure you want me to go in that place right there?"

"Yes, now go! The sooner you get with the program, the sooner we can finish all of this craziness you are wanting us to do. So go!" Ian repeats himself to Mason.

Mason stands up, his smile gets bigger as he turns and walks over to the door closest to them, the one Ian instructed him to go to for water. Mason opens the door, and the loud sounds of people singing, fighting, and cheering roll out into the alley. He swiftly closes the wooden door behind him as he enters.

"What kind of a place did you just send Mason into?" Kenzie as Ian.

"I'm not sure, but you need water, and that door is the closest," Ian admits.

"Well, I hope he doesn't have too much of a good time in there. It sounds like there is a party going there right now," Kenzie tells Ian.

"Here, slide up against this wall, and save your strength until Masson brings you something to drink. He shouldn't be too much longer if he is serious about his plans," Ian tries to relax Kenzie while leaning her up against the wall.

About that time, Mason comes shooting out of the same door he had just entered, holding a glass of what looks like some dirty water. He walks over to where Ian and Kenzie are, and hands the murky glass of water to Kenzie.

"What in the world is in this glass? There is no way that this is water. Did you scoop that up out of a toilet?" Ian asks Mason while placing one hand over the top of the glass in Kenzie's hand to ensure she does not take a drink of it until he says it's okay.

"Let's just say this, it is the weakest kind of water they serve there, so I would not drink it fast, or very much of it," Mason gives them both a look of, 'you asked for it.'

Ian looks at Kenzie and nods for her to take a slow sip of the brew that is in her glass.

Kenzie raises the obscured glass to her nose to smell it first, then crinkles her nose and takes a small sip of the liquid in the glass. With just one small sip, Kenzie spits it back out all over Mason. Not only does she spit it out, but has a nasty cough behind it.

"Are you trying to kill me? What in the world was that?" Kenzie asks Mason.

"Well, during these times, that is called 'fire water.' It's whiskey! Sorry, but a saloon does not serve water during this time period," Mason reports with a laugh. "We will have to get you some water from somewhere else. So do you think you have enough energy for us to get out of this ally and get to where we need to go?"

"Do you think you could make it just to the outskirts of town?" Ian asks Kenzie.

"I'm going to do my best. I am ready to get this over with," Kenzie expresses to Ian.

"Okay, Mason, can you help me carry Kenzie with us? You put one of her arms over your shoulders and I will do the same with the other. We will all just have to walk together at the same pace that will not put too much stress on Kenzie," Ian instructs Mason.

Ian and Mason gather Kenzie and once they have a secure hold of her, they all begin to walk together. They are heading out of the alley, as if Ian knows where he needs to go, which brings suspicion to Mason.

"And just how do you know where we are supposed to be going? Is this a memory you have visited before?" Mason asked.

"No, not this memory, but I do know when we are and where Sebastian and Grayson could be right now. If they are not together yet, they will be soon," Ian defines his knowledge of this place they are at.

"Well, lead the way," Mason says with enthusiasm.

"It's this way, and don't worry, it's not too far out," Ian tells them as he begins to lead the way to the West of the ally. Once they are at the end of the alley, Ian suggests they turn North, or right that is.

They walk only a few blocks before they reach the edge of the small town. This, of course, is very strange to all three of them. Well, mostly to Ian and Mason, as they were born and raised in the New York and Brooklyn area. Kenzie's hometown of Enloe was much smaller than this one, and the town she went to school in, Cooper, Texas, was really not much bigger, so she was still in a little shock.

"It's not much further now, we just need to walk through this field here and try to catch them at their favorite spot down by the creek," Ian reports to the others.

Kenzie's eyes lit up like a Christmas Tree. The first thing that comes to her mind is WATER! Being from the country, she is not afraid of a little creek water. The thought alone was enough to put a pep in her step.

Now that Kenzie can walk with a quick step, the three of them are able to sneak up on Sebastian sitting alone on the creek bed. He must be waiting on Grayson.

"Perfect timing," Mason whispers to Ian. "Now is your chance to go out there and convince your relative that it will be in all of your best interests to give all of his powers to the 'Time Keeper' and all the information about it to Grayson when he shows up."

"Do you really think this is the best time? What if Grayson walks up in the middle of me talking with Sebastian? How do you suppose I explain who I am and what I am doing here? Also, the first thing we need to do is to get Kenzie is some of that creek water. She has to drink something before she dehydrates." Ian replies.

"Ian is right, Mason. I have to get some fluids in me before I pass out again and need medical attention before any of us can leave here," Kenzie informs Mason of just how bad her condition is.

"Well, why don't you go and make some chit-chat with your relative Sebastian, and I will walk Kenzie upstream a little bit, so she can get some water without being seen or heard by you down there? Then when we come back, we can make our presence noticeable and run interference with Grayson, if and when he shows up," Masons suggest an alternative plan.

"That sounds like at least an attempt at a plan. What do you think, Kenzie?" Ian asks.

"I think it's the best we can come up with right now. I don't anticipate going too long. Just a few gallons of water and I should be back to normal in no time. I say there are risks we are going to have to take," Kenzie agrees with Mason's plan.

"Then why don't you two go ahead and start making your way up the creek, and I'll head down to try to convince Sebastian that this is the best thing for both of our families. Let's just hope I can be convincing enough for him to believe me," Ian tells Mason and Kenzie.

"You better find a way to make him believe you because you and Kenzie have a lot riding on this. So you better make it happen," Mason reminds them of what's at stake for them if they fail.

"Just go with Kenzie right now and let me deal with my family relatives," Ian spits out back to Mason.

Mason shakes his head at Ian while taking on more weight from Kenzie. They begin to walk upstream as quietly as possible until they can find a safe location for Kenzie to be able to get her water.

***

As Kenzie and Mason take off, leaving Ian with Sebastian, Ian takes a deep breath. Then he begins his walk down to the creek edge to speak to Sebastian. But just as he can exit the bushes that he has been hiding in, he hears a voice call out a name.

"Sebastian, are you here? Did you beat me here again? How do you do it?" It's Grayson coming down the edge of the creek, smiling and waving at Sebastian.

Now, what am I supposed to do? I was prepared to talk to just Sebastian, not both of them, Ian thinks to himself. *I am just going to have to see what happens.*

Ian starts his move out of the bushes for the second time.

"Excuse me, but are you, Sebastian Helen and Grayson Zimmerman?" Ian asks politely as possible.

Sebastian and Grayson both pull out their sidearms and say, "Depends on who you are and why you are asking! It better be good if you plan on living," Grayson says to Ian.

Ian does not remember the pair of them being violent to anyone, except to each other, so he is frozen and left with his mouth wide open. The fear on his face is enough to convince Sebastian that Ian means no harm.

Sebastian lowers his sidepiece and puts his hand on Grayson's. He motions for him to lower his as well. "Look at him, Grayson. He's just a scared kid. Put that thing away."

Grayson takes a hard look at Ian and starts laughing while placing his sidearm back into its holster on his hip. "Boy, we really had you scared. You would think you never had a gun pulled on you before. Where in this world can someone live and not have a gun pulled on them for one reason or another, even at your age?" Grayson mocks Ian.

With a sigh of relief, Ian relaxes. "Let's say you are correct and that I am not from these parts. But I am glad the two of you are together because there are a few things we need to discuss and are going to be hard for you two to understand," Ian tells Sebastian and Grayson.

"Okay, son, you have our attention," Sebastian lets Ian know.

"First, I need to be honest with you both. I am not here alone. I have two companions with me, but one of them, Kenzie, needed water before she dehydrated, so Mason, the other person with us, took her upstream to get a drink from the creek. They should be back soon. I want you both to know none of us are here to hurt you or do you any harm. We are only here to talk. All of our futures will depend on what happens after our talk. Okay?" Ian advises them of Mason and Kenzie.

"Okay, but the first sign of a double-cross, and we will start shooting. You get my meaning, don't you?" Grayson tells Ian as a 'matter of fact'.

"Of course. I would expect nothing less from you both. Now, I will go ahead and begin, and when my friends get here, they can verify what I'm asking of you," Ian begins explaining why they are there.

***

Mason and Kenzie walk a little way upstream until it begins to open up to a clear field.

"We should stop here and get your water. If we get out in the open, we are sure to be seen by a farmer or someone," Mason tells Kenzie, who agrees with him.

With both of them being in agreeance, Mason makes his way down to the bank of the creek as gently as possible while taking on most of Kenzie's weight. Once they are both on the creek bed, Kenzie drops to her knees and begins to cup water up to her mouth, using her hands. Kenzie continues this process, only stopping to take a breath in between handfuls of water going into her body.

Kenzie is already feeling better and feeling her power and strength coming back after about ten minutes of drinking the creek water. Kenzie continues for about five more minutes before she looks up at Mason and thanks him.

"You are welcome?" Mason says back to Kenzie, unsure why the young girl he has kidnapped and forced to take him back in time, is thanking him for helping her to get some water.

Mason helps Kenzie up from the creek bed with less help as needed before. No words are exchanged between the two of them. Once they are back on the bank of the creek, they begin their walk back to where they left Ian to speak to Sebastian.

As they get closer to Ian's location, they can hear Ian trying to explain what he needs from Sebastian. As they get closer, they can hear a third voice. Who is that?" Kenzie asks Mason.

"I think it must be Grayson."

"We need to get in there with Ian right now," Kenzie says urgently to Mason.

"And how do you expect us to do that? Just storm down there and interrupt them? Do you not see, they both have guns in their holsters?" Mason clarifies.

"I'll freeze them, then we can make our move," Kenzie replies.

"You can't freeze them, Kenzie. Remember what happened when you tried to freeze your parents Jerry and Delores Green?"

"Those weren't my parents, and you know that," Kenzie barks back at Mason, just a little too loud.

"You can't freeze anything that is not from your time period. That is all I am trying to tell you."

Kenzie is about to say something more to Mason, then stops when she hears Ian call their names.

***

"That is why we need you, Sebastian, to try and transfer your powers to the 'Time Keeper' over to Grayson," Ian stops short.

"What was that noise? It sounds like it came from over yonder, in those weeds," Grayson says.

"I think that must be my friends. Kenzie, is that you?" Ian gives a little shout.

"Um, yes. Who else would be hiding in the bushes?"

"Well, you and Mason can come out, slowly. Also, keep your hands visible at all times. They are a trusting pair, but still are precautious," Ian instructs Mason and Kenzie.

They come out of the bushes, slowly with their hands held out in front of them. As they walk towards Ian, they notice Sebastian and Grayson, standing with their hands on their undrawn sidearms. They continue, slowly until they make it down to Ian's location, then they put their hands down.

"So, these are the other two from the future with you?" Grayson asks Ian.

"Yes, this is Kenzie, and that is a great-relative of yours, Mason," Ian fills them in.

"What all did you have time to tell them while we were getting water?" Kenzie asks.

"They are all caught up and ready to try to transfer the powers over. I explained to them what's at stake for us if they don't try, and Sebastian is willing to give up the power of the 'Time Keeper' if it can possibly save his future family and yours, Mason," Ian tells Kenzie and Mason what they missed while they were getting Kenzie water from upstream.

"So, that's it? Sebastian is just going to give up the powers, just like that?" Mason asks in disbelief.

"Yes, Mason. Just as important as your family in the future is important to you, Sebastian's family in the future is just as important to him. That makes him willing to try anything to keep them safe. And just so you know, Grayson was harder to convince to do this. He does not want the responsibility of what could be lost in our future because of your selfishness, but he too cares about family. Even if it's not his, he's trying to save," Ian expresses to Mason.

"Well, Grayson, I'm sorry you have no clue what life is for your future relatives because the 'Time Keeper' was used inappropriately over the years by Sebastian. You get to show everyone how to be responsible with such a great gift and save us all," Mason tells Grayson with glee.

"This is where we will never agree. You don't know anything about me, or can you be sure I will not make the same decisions Sebastian makes or will make," Grayson expresses back to Mason with sorrow.

"Enough of this chit-chat, and let the transfer of powers begin. I have not spent my entire life to get to this moment just to walk away now," Mason demands.

"Fine. Sebastian, when you are ready, I need you to hold the 'Time Keeper' with one hand, and you hold the other end with your hand, Grayson. Once you both have a firm hold on the 'Time Keeper,' Sebastian, I need you to connect to the 'Time Keeper,' and at the same time, think of Grayson and try to pull him into the 'Time Keeper.' As you are pulling him in, try releasing yourself from it, along with your powers. It's going to be like walking away from something you don't want. Are you both ready?" Ian directs the two best friends for the transfer of powers of the 'Time Keeper.'

Sebastian and Grayson do as he is instructed, both holding one end of the 'Time Keeper' at the same time. Sebastian closes his eyes, and Grayson does as well. Sebastian does as he is instructed until he feels the power of the 'Time Keeper' leave his body, and he feels like the 'Time Keeper' actually kick him out and makes his hand let go of his end of the 'Time Keeper' he was holding.

On the other end, Grayson feels a surge of power shooting through him as he connects to the 'Time Keeper.'

"Did it work?" Mason asks Grayson.

"I think so. I feel an odd power and connection to this watch. Now, what do I do?" Grayson asks Mason.

"Just live your life. Now we have to leave you and go back to our time to beat any time ripples that may happen due to the transfer. It was such a pleasure meeting you both, and thank you again," Mason tells Grayson and Sebastian as he looks over at Ian, as to let him know they need to leave, and NOW!

Mason and Ian both grab Kenzie's hands, take a deep breath, and then they vanish right in front of Sebastian and Grayson.

***

Kenzie, Ian, and Mason reappear, but this time they are in Mason's office. It seems as if the powers of the 'Time Keeper' have been transferred over to Mason through the generations of Grayson's bloodline.

As Mason notices where they are, he releases himself from Kenzie and runs to his safe. Mason presses the buttons on his safe so fast he messes up the code twice. Before Mason can panic, he takes a deep breath, relaxes, and slows his heart rate down. Once he is more relaxed, he tries the safe code one more time, and this time the light turns from red to green. Mason smiles and turns the handle of the safe. To his surprise, his brother's old coins, the lock of hair belonging to his baby sister, and his mother's journal are all missing. The only thing left in the safe regarding his family is a photo.

Mason is afraid to even look at the photo, but he knows he has to. Mason reaches into the safe and retrieves the photo. The first thing he notices is there are no dates on the back. This sends cold chills down his spine and hopes that everything worked out as planned. Mason quickly turns the photo over, expecting to see the photo of his entire family, his mom, dad, baby sister, brother, and himself. But to his surprise, everyone is in the photo, except him.

"What is the meaning of this?" Mason is furious with Ian and Kenzie.

"We told you not to mess with the past. Now you see why messing with the past is never a good thing, no matter how good your intentions are. But look at it this way, you won't be beaten by your father, and you won't have to suffer losing your mother, brother, and sister now," Ian tells Mason.

"Kenzie get us out of here! NOW!" Ian yells as he is still holding her hand. Then, poof, they vanish, leaving Mason alone in his 'perfect' new future he created for himself.

***

In the middle of Connor throwing two of the guards down the hallway, Ian and Kenzie suddenly appear right in the middle of all the ensuing battle going on at the compound.

"What in the world is going on here?" Ian shouts.

"We are attacking the compound until you could get back," Connor replies.

"Connor, I need something big enough to make a portal for all of us to fit through. Is Kayla and everyone else here?" Ian asks.

"Yes, we are all here and ready to go!" Connor shouts as he is in the process of moving the largest part of the polished marble floor upright and against the wall of the hallway. "Will this work for you, Ian?"

"You bet it will. Now can you all cover me while I make us a portal to get us to the school?" Ian shouts as he prepares to work his powers on the shining marble flooring, now leaning on the wall.

It only takes Ian a few seconds to create the portal. Then he calls Kayla, Kenzie, Jax, Garrett, Maria, and Connor through the portal.

"What about Maclaine?" Maria asks Ian.

"What about who?"

"Maclaine is on our side. He needs to come with us. He will be punished if we leave him here."

"Fine, Maclaine, get over here and walk through this portal, NOW!" Ian exclaims.

As soon as everyone has made it through the portal, Ian steps through and closes it before anyone else can come through.

Chapter 17

Ian's Mission?

Once Ian crossed through the portal, the one made in the large portion of the freshly polished marble floor from the compound, the one Connor moved for Ian to use, he closes it and Connor is able to break the flooring piece they used at the same time, on the other side of the portal before it closed.

"Wow, that was a close call," Brayden says out loud to everyone.

"Mason is going to be so mad. Where is Mason by the way? I couldn't help but notice he is not with you and Kenzie in the compound hallway when you appeared," Maria asks.

"We will never have to worry about Mason ever again if things went the way they were supposed to. Right, Ian?" Jax wonders with a smile.

"How can you smile at a time like this Jax? Mason now has the powers of the 'Time Keeper' thanks to us. Even though he may not have them much longer, who knows what other damage he can do while he does have the powers to the 'Time Keeper,'" Kenzie suggests.

"You mean to tell me that you were able to actually go back in time and have Sebastian transfer his powers over the 'Time Keeper' to Grayson?" Maria sounds shocked. "That is not supposed to even be possible."

"How could you do what Mason wanted you to do in the first place? There is no telling what time ripples are going to be caused now!" Kayla says. "Am I even back in this timeline, because I don't feel any different?"

"Wait, you don't understand what Jax means," Ian tries to calm down the crowd.

"Then answer the question. Where is Mason, and why would he not have much time left with the 'Time Keeper's powers," Garrett demands to know.

"Well, that's easy. We went back in time, forced Sebastian to give his powers to Grayson to save Connor's and all of your lives, and then we teleported to Mason's office. He opened his safe and found some photos of his family. Well, it was a family photo without him. Then we left Mason there and teleported to y'all in the hallway," Kenzie sums up their events.

"Is this true, Ian?" Maclaine asks.

"I told you we never should have sent Ian and Kenzie with Mason," Brayden speaks for once.

"No, you didn't. You never said anything," Connor replies.

"Would you all just stop for a minute to let me explain? Please. First, Kayla, you are not back in our timeline yet. We are still trying to figure that part out. Sorry. We are going to keep trying to get you back here with us," Ian tells everyone, especially Kayla.

"I know you will never give up, Ian," Kayla tells Ian with hope.

"Now, the second thing is that Mason does not have the powers of the 'Time Keeper,' and he never did. The memory we took Mason was a fake one, made up by the Chancellor of the Believers herself, Billie June. Jax was able to inform me of this fake memory trap for Mason as we were teleporting to the compound. The same way I spoke to Junior when Kenzie teleported us to find Jax, who just happened to be with the Headmaster and Chancellor Billie June. That's why Jax was there, Kenzie. They were coming up with a nonlethal way to remove Mason from our timeline, so he could never hurt anyone ever again."

"Then if the memory is fake, then where did we leave Mason?" Kenzie asks in surprise.

"Mason is stuck in a time loop, created by the Chancellor at the Believers Headquarters. He is in the large room, fit for a King. I was shown by Junior in my dreams before. The one with the large fireplace and red wallpaper. Jax even stayed in that same room when he visited the Chancellor, didn't you, Jax? Mason is now living in a loop of a time ripple removing him from the timeline for three seconds, then starts back over when the three of us appear in what he thinks is his office, alive, but not so well," Ian finishes.

"So, you still have the 'Time Keeper' and its powers?" Maria asks.

"Yes, I never lost them. Mason just thought I did because that is what he wanted to happen. It was an ingenious memory loop and trap," Ian replies.

"I'm so glad to hear that. I know how to get Kayla back in our timeline, but you are going to have to access the 'Time Keeper' to do it. You will also need the silver ring back and the puzzle piece Kayla has been hiding. So if you don't mind, could you please give those things over to Ian, Kayla?" Maria brings forth some light for the end of their tunnel.

"How do you know I have those things, Maria?"

"Kayla, I am not the only person who has been helping Ian find a way to bring you back to our current timeline. You are a very important part of the future. Therefore, many people have been helping Ian without either of your knowledge to bring you back. Please, I beg of you to trust me now more than ever. I would not have come this far just to keep you out of history," Maria tells Kayla.

"Who else has been helping us?" Ian asks Maria.

"Right now, that does not matter. But getting those items from Kayla does, and me telling you what you need to do with them does. We still don't have much time. Time ripples are still affecting the future without Kayla in it," Maria stresses.

"And just what do you have to gain from all of this? Besides getting to quit working with Mason?" Ian asks.

"I also get part of my family back. You see, I was chosen for this mission after Kenzie and Connor's mother's mind was erased, along with their father's. They were stolen because their mother is my sister. Kenzie and Connor are my niece and nephew. My hope is, that once this is completed, everything will go back to normal as if Mason never messed with any of our families." Maria wipes tears from her eyes while looking at Kenzie and Connor, as she finishes her reasoning for agreeing to do this missing for the Believers. "I'm so sorry about not being able to rescue you from the Greens. By the time I even found out who they were, you had already found a brilliant way to escape on your own. Just like your mother would have, Kenzie."

"If you are our aunt, why are you just now telling us? You have had plenty of chances to tell any of us about this. So why now?" Kenzie questions.

"I am sorry, but I couldn't blow my cover until we had Mason trapped. If he had found out the truth, he would have killed all three of us. It was kept a secret for all of our protection. I promise," Maria reassures Kenzie and Connor.

"Kenzie give Maria a break. We all have had to do things that we are not proud of or even wanted to do, but we did it for the safety of our family. I believe her, and I can tell she is telling the truth," Connor tells Kenzie.

"How can you trust her after all that she has done? How can you tell she is telling the truth?" Kenzie asks Connor.

"Let's just say it's a gift I have," is all Connor would say.

"Fine, Connor, I will trust you for now," Kenzie embraces Connor's possible new gift. "Well, go ahead, Maria, finish what you were telling about how to bring Kayla back to our timeline and save history."

"Thank you, Connor and Kenzie. I am so thankful we are back together and soon to have my sister, your real mother, and your father, back. But you are correct Kenzie, Ian has a very important trip to make. Now, Kayla, have you got those items I requested for Ian to use?"

"Yes, Maria, I have already given them both to Ian," Kayla remarks.

"Thank you. Now, if you are ready, Ian, I can explain what you need to do with the puzzle piece and ring," Maria tells Ian.

"I hate to interrupt this family reunion and mission, but there is something I need to tell you all," Garrett interrupts Maria.

"And just want can you add to all of this, Garrett?" Brayden asks.

"I can't tell everyone about myself or how I came upon what I am about to tell you. I will not answer any questions, so please don't ask any. But from what I understand, this is a very important part of Ian's mission," Garrett replies to Brayden.

"Okay, you have our attention. Now, get on with it," Ian tells Garrett.

"Kayla is not the only person with a puzzle piece. I was also given one when I was told to join Mason's group. I was not told anything about it, except it is the most important part of my mission. So, either two pieces are missing from the same puzzle, or these are two puzzles missing one piece each. I guess Ian will need my puzzle piece as well, just in case the place you are sending Ian to is missing two pieces instead of just one," Garrett explains.

"You have had a puzzle piece this entire time and never told me about it, even though you knew I had one? Did you think it was a coincidence that we both had a puzzle piece?" Kayla goes off on Garrett.

"Wait, the two of you know each other? Why is this the first time we have heard about this?" Maria asks.

"First, Kayla, I'm sorry I could not tell you, I could not risk the future changing any more than it has already. Second, Maria, there has been too much going on for me to make you aware of all my adventures. I have been helping in many ways. In ways you could never understand. Which leads me to also believe that Mason has someone helping him as well," Garrett explains.

"I have been around Mason enough to know that he has no other friends, or even visitors, other than those in the compound. There is no way he could be getting help from someone," Maria is confident in her assumption.

"Let's just say this type of help he has been receiving is not really the 'in person' or 'phone call' type of person," Garrett says.

"You mean he's getting help from someone from the future. Someone like ..." Kayla stops.

"The future? That would be the only way he could always be one step ahead of us. It was like he always knew what we were going to do before we did it. But how would you know someone from the future could still be here, Kayla?" Maria asks.

"I'm sorry, but I can't tell you that. It is the only logical explanation of how Mason knew so much," Kenzie replies.

"This is all fascinating stuff, but, Maria, did you say we don't have much time? If so, then the rest of this can wait. Right now, Ian needs to know what to do with those two puzzle pieces and his silver ring," Connor insists.

"Connor is correct, Maria. I need to know what I need to do. Kayla is my priority right now. If you have the answers, then it's time you give them to me," Ian steps in.

"What I am about to tell you is going to be a hard mission for you because you have to go and do this one on your own. Do you think you will be able to complete this mission alone? You will have no help from any of us or any way to call for help either," Maria gives Ian more details about his mission.

"Yes, I believe I am strong and smart enough to be able to look for a puzzle piece or two in this mission."

"Then let's begin with where and when you will need to go back in time. And yes, you are the only one who can do this because it's the first memory stored in the 'Time Keeper' by its creator, Peter Hele. This memory of his goes back to the 15th Century. You are going to have to think hard and use as much power as you can to enter this memory. Once you enter Peter's memory, you can move around and look for his workshop. It's said that he did all of his work there. Not just the work on watches, but also other projects he attempted, such as new inventions, or even a puzzle to relax his mind," Maria takes a pause.

"Well, that does not sound difficult so far. I am not hearing anything too challenging," Ian tells Maria. "I do have a question though. What is supposed to happen when the puzzle, or puzzles, are completed? How will I know I have completed the correct puzzles and the mission?"

"Well, that part is unclear. Since something like this has never happened before, no one knows how you will know when you have succeeded, but we do know you will know. Power like that will leave some kind of mark or force. Some sort of energy surge that will be strong enough for all of us to feel through time."

"Well, that's pretty vague, don't you think? Will I be able to feel the same surge of power?"

"Yes, you should feel it harder than any of us. You will be right in the epicenter, which will cause the surge."

"Are you all sure this will only bring Kayla back and not mess up the timeline or future any more than Mason already has?"

"We were very confident until now. Finding out there are two puzzle pieces sort of puts some confusion on things. We thought the one Kayla had was the piece of her future to be put back. But now with two pieces, we don't know who the other history belongs to. We are sure Kayla will be back, so are you ready to get started?" Maria asks Ian for one last, 'Yes'.

"Not just yet. You still have not told me what I need to do with the silver ring," Ian replies to Maria.

"Oh yes, that is a very important part of this. But now comes new possible complications," Maria stops.

"What kind of complications?"

"In the beginning, you were supposed to put the ring back on your ring finger just before you pressed the puzzle piece in place. But since we have two puzzle pieces and possibly two separate puzzles missing a piece, things are different now. That means you will have to pick one of the two puzzles to put the ring on your finger when pressing in the puzzle piece. You will only know which one to choose when you get there."

"Don't worry, Ian. I know you will figure something out and do the right thing," Kayla gives Ian a boost of confidence.

Ian takes a look around the room, taking in the faces of all his new friends and his best friend Kayla, and hopes what he is about to do works. He does not want anything to happen to any of these people he now calls 'family'.

"I'm ready, Maria. What do I need to do to access the first memory of Peter Hele's?"

"Close your eyes and let your mind sift through the memories in the 'Time Keeper' until you feel you have found the one you are looking for. You will know the one."

Ian closes his eyes, holding the two puzzle pieces, one in each hand and the ring from Kayla in his right hand, and begins to let his mind wander through the memories in the 'Time Keeper'.

***

"What is the meaning of this?" Mason is furious with Ian and Kenzie for about the four hundredth time in his time loop trap. Except, this time, Ian and Kenzie are not there to answer him, but his mother is.

"Hello, Mason," his mother speaks to him softly.

"Mom? Is that really you?" Mason asks in disbelief.

"Yes, son, it's your mother. I know it's been a very long time, but I am here for only a few minutes. There are some things I need to remind you about.

Do you remember the last entry in my journal and what I wrote?"

"Yes, mother. I read it every year, but nothing changes. It always says the same thing, and I have been doing what you told me to do this entire time. I'm sorry I keep failing you," Mason says with tears falling from his eyes.

"You see, this is what I am here to remind you. I also said, '...that you can't let the past consume you. You will have to move forward with your lives, just as if the next day is not guaranteed, like your father and I did. That will be the only way you will have no regrets in life. You will have a life full of love, laughter, tears, smiles, friends, and even some failures. There is nothing wrong with failing because you tried.' Do you remember those words, Mason?"

"But you also said, 'If you fail, learn from your mistakes, and try again, but keep trying,' remember those words, mother?"

"You seem to have left off the most important part of that last sentence you almost quoted correctly and that is, 'and moving on.' Simply meaning if you fail, learn from it, keep trying from what you learned, but also keep moving on with your life. You have only been focused on one aspect of my note to you. And now you see what happens when you go too far. You see now who's being removed from time, don't you?

"The reason I am telling you this is because you are now entering your final hour of learning from your mistakes. Open your heart and mind up to the rest of my letter to you. Once you can accept that we are gone and move on with your life, you will break this loop and live a life full of all those things missing from it now. Love, laughter, tears, smiles, friends, and even more failures you can learn from.

"But if you fail this time, in this final hour, you will not get the chance to try again. You will be erased from history, and it will be because of your own doing. So, please sit and think about that, but not too long. I want you to have the life I wrote for you to have.

"I'm sorry, but I have to go now. I have faith you can do the right thing. I love you, son," are the last words before Mason's mother disappears, leaving him with an hour to figure out what he wants to do. Accept that his mother and siblings are gone and move on with his life, or be willing to be erased from history because he refuses to stop believing he can bring her back.

***

As Ian peeks into so many memories the 'Time Keeper' has stored in it over the centuries by his relatives, he can't help but see the amazing things his family has done in the past. Then, for a split second his memories change to a completely new family.

Confused by this new unknown family he is seeing and feeling, Ian slows down the memory search. He wants to find out who these people are and how they were able to store memories in the 'Time Keeper'.

As he watches more of this memory, Ian begins to understand that he is also accessing the memories stored in the silver ring. The ring was forged with a small piece of the 'Time Keeper'. It was given to Camryn's father, who melted it into a silver ring. He then gave it to his wife, Jennifer, on the day of their child's christening. He explained that Camryn should get it when she becomes of age, and it is to be passed down from female to female for generations to come. Her husband never told anyone else in their family about it, so they didn't understand why he was so adamant with his instructions, but he was.

This is when Ian remembers the story Jax told Kenzie and himself about a young Chancellor Billie June breaking the laws of the Believers for what she believed to be the right thing to do. Then it all clicked. That is why he needs to put the ring on as he presses in the puzzle piece given to him by Kayla. It's her family and his family's bloodlines in that ring together!

Then Ian feels that there is another memory he is meant to go to, one belonging to the 'Time Keeper'. So he shifts his attention back to his original purpose, to find the original memory saved by Peter Hele in the 'Time Keeper'.

Upon leaving the ring's memory and returning to the 'Time Keeper's memories, he knows he is in the original memory. He knows because he feels he can't go any further back, and his body is telling him that also.

Ian has no other choice but to stop his memory travel there or get off the memory train so to speak.

As Ian begins to walk around in the very first memory of Peter Hele's, the creator of the watch, he can't help but feel like he is in the memory of royalty. But he quickly lets that feeling pass because he knows he's on a time-sensitive matter. He has to find Peter's workshop.

Ian begins his search in Peter's bedroom. This is where the first memory was stored. Even if it was by mistake, it was still stored in the 'Time Keeper'. So now, Ian has to go out into the rest of the house to find a workshop. Ian has no idea how big, or small, Peter's house is. The only way for him to find out is to open the bedroom door and sneak around until he finds the workshop. So, Ian makes his way over to the bedroom door, grabs the doorknob, twists it, and pulls it open.

To his surprise, the home is a modest home, with only a few rooms from what he can see from the bedroom door. It looks to be a single floor home, which is great for Ian. The fewer floors mean fewer rooms he has to check, making it quicker for him to find Peter's workshop.

Ian leaves Peter's bedroom, closing the door behind himself, and begins to walk around the one-story home. It does not sound like anyone is home, as all is quiet. Ian decides not to check the other doors along the hallway, as they are more than likely more bedrooms. He focuses on doors in other parts of the house. He checks closet doors, pantry doors, and even back doors to the house, never finding a workshop.

Finally, Ian thinks he could have been wrong about the doors in the hallway being all bedroom doors. *Maybe one of those doors is Peter Hele's workshop, and not a bedroom at all,* Ian thinks to himself. So Ian rushes back to the original hallway and starts opening the doors, one by one. All revealing nothing more than a bedroom.

Perplexed, Ian finds himself back in Peter Hele's bedroom. The place where he started. *Why am I back in this room? I have already been here, and it's nothing more than his bedroom,* Ian thinks again to himself.

As Ian sits on Peter's bed, knowing he is running out of time, he notices a light shining under the closet door. Ian moves over from the bed and opens the closet door. He finds the light is not coming directly from inside the closet but through a false door at the back. Ian's surprise of a secret door leading to a secret room excited him. From what he knew about 15th Century Germany, not many small homes had secret rooms or passages built during that time. He finds out later that Peter's modest home was once part of a large castle built in the 10th Century mostly destroyed during the wars between the Hanseatic League and the Danes in 1361A.D. This war lasted nine years and was won by the Hanseatic League when they conquered Copenhagen and ended with the Treaty of Stralsund.

Ian moves to the back of the closet and pulls the false door away from the wall, revealing a spiral staircase leading down to a basement type room. Ian begins his descent down the stairs after he places the false door back, closing off the entrance to this secret room. Once Ian has made it to the bottom of the stairs, he stops and takes a look around, taking it all in. He's found Peter Hele's workshop.

Once the amazement settles in with Ian, he quickly remembers he's looking for one puzzle missing two puzzle pieces or two puzzle pieces missing one piece each. Ian begins to move around the room. He only sees bits and pieces of the makings of watches or clocks, but no puzzles. *Now, where can the puzzles be? Where could he be hiding them?* Ian thinks to himself.

Then just out of the corner of his eye, he notices a small table in the corner of the room, maybe where Peter ate while working in his workshop, but this time it is covered with a large picture. Ian runs over to the table. Low and behold, it's not a picture, but a puzzle of a Red Cardinal, a puzzle missing two puzzle pieces to complete it.

"YES! I FOUND IT!" Ian exclaims out loud as he places his hand on the puzzle to make sure it is real.

"Who's down there?" Ian hears a voice call from the top of the spiral staircase.

Ian does not say a word but grabs both of the puzzle pieces and sets them right on top of their rightful places to the puzzle, both looking to fit and finish this puzzle. He presses the silver ring on his right ring finger and pushes the puzzle pieces down at the same time into the puzzle.

Just as both puzzle pieces fill their spots in the puzzle of Peter Hele's, not only does Ian feel a large surge of power, but he sees the brightest light he has ever seen. The force of the power surge and the light is so strong they throw Ian back against the wall nearest the table, knocking him out cold.

Chapter 18

Reality?

As he hits the wall, due to the force of the power surge, all Ian's memories begin to flash forward in his mind. He does not know for how many days he has been knocked out. As he tries to open his eyes, he still sees the bright light.

"Kayla, did it work?" Ian begins speaking, still unsure of where he is. He figured that once he finished the puzzle, he would be sent back to the school with the rest of his team, Kayla, Connor, Brayden, Garrett, Maclaine, Jax, Kenzie, and Maria.

"What are you trying to say, Ian?" his mother asks.

"Mom? What are you doing here at the school?"

"Try not to talk too much, Ian. You are very sick. You are in a hospital Intensive Care Unit. You have been here for almost two weeks suffering from Delirium," a nearby doctor interjects for Ian's mother.

"Nurses give Ian another sedative for now. We need to run some more tests on him, now that he is awake and responsive," the doctor orders a nurse standing next to Ian in his hospital bed. The next thing Ian knows, he is asleep again.

***

Ian begins to open his eyes again. This time the bright light is not shining in his eyes, making it easier for him to open them. He takes a look around and can tell he is back at the school with his friends around him, which relaxes Ian very much.

"Kayla? Are you here?" Ian asks in a more demanding tone.

"Yes, Ian. I am here, and so is everyone else.

"What happened? And why didn't you answer me last time, Kayla? Did it work? Are you back in our timeline and in the future?" Ian asks with confusion.

"What do you mean, 'last time'? This is the first time you have been awake since you successfully completed the mission. You, completing the puzzle with both puzzle pieces, worked. I am back now in our time line and will make it to the future. All thanks to you," Kayla expresses with gratitude to Ian.

"Where did my mom go? She was here a few minutes ago. I could hear her voice saying I was sick," Ian says to everyone standing around him.

"Sick? Ian, your mother is still in Brooklyn. She has not been to the school, as most parents are not allowed," Jax answers Ian's question.

"Then how did I hear her? And where was I when I first woke up? They said I was in a hospital ICU, sick. Then I went back to sleep and woke up here with you all. So what is going on here?"

"Maybe you need more rest, Ian. Why don't we let you take a nap in your room for a little bit, and we can check on you later? How does that sound?" Maria asks Ian, not expecting an answer.

"How did we get in my room?" Ian inquires right before falling asleep.

***

"Ian, can you hear me? It's mom," Ian's mother asks with concern.

Ian mumbles incoherently back to his mother, but he does not open his eyes.

"Dr, what's wrong with him? Why is he not getting any better? He has been here for almost two weeks," she asks.

"I know you are worried about Ian right now, but you have to understand that this is a new virus that no one has ever seen before, much less know how to treat. We are in the middle of a pandemic with this virus and still learning about it. We are only able to check for specific symptoms for this virus. Your son has had them earlier this year before testing was available. It is highly likely he has already had the virus, not once but twice, and somehow fought it off. We think that since he caught it twice in just a little over a thirty-day period, he may have had double the antibodies, or they could have been just the first two strains, which we are learning are not as harmful to the patients. It seems to be affecting people over sixty-five years old and only a very few cases of under twenty-one years old.

"Now, when Ian lost his taste and smell, back in March from what we believe was his second infection of this virus, it did not come back until two weeks ago. Up until then, he was able to eat or drink anything he wanted. But when his taste and smell did return for him, everything came back with the most horrible state and smell he could imagine. He was able to force himself to eat, drink, and take his medication for his ADHD, ASD, and KLS, for one week. But after that week, he could no longer tolerate the taste or smell of anything. That caused him to be unable to eat, drink, or even take his medication for seven straight days, causing him to dehydrate. While being dehydrated, his body naturally produced lithium. His body overproduced the amount of lithium his body could take, causing him to have lithium toxicity. That is what is causing his delirium now. He is suffering from a psychiatric break from reality and fantasy. He does not know what is real or fake at this moment.

"We figured that once we reduced the amount of lithium his body produced back to normal, he would get better. But for some reason, that's not the case here. We have been keeping him sedated for the past two days," the doctor explains to Ian's mother.

"Well, if you have had him sedated for the past two days, and his lithium levels are normal now, how do you know he is still having a psychotic break?" Ian's mother asks in reply to the doctor's clinical diagnosis of Ian.

"Because when his sedation wears off, he begins shouting names like Kayla, Mason, Maria, Connor, Kenzie, Jax, the list goes on. Do any of these names sound familiar to you? Are they family members or friends of Ian's?" the doctor asks.

"Well, Kayla is his best friend that lives in our building. They have known each other and grown up together, but the rest of the names I have not heard him mention before."

"Well, he gets very agitated at several of the names, needless to say. We have had two nurses named Maria resign from helping with Ian due to the things he would say to them. Let's say it was not the politest thing one could say to another, but they also knew that it was not Ian, but the virus causing him to think he was someone else, or somewhere else at the time," the doctor explained in more detail.

Ian can hear what is going on around him, but unable to react. The more he tries to communicate with his mother or the doctor, the more exhausted he becomes, and back into a deep sleep he goes.

***

Ian shoots up in his bed, the one back at the school. He is so confused. He believes he is being torn between two alternate worlds or timelines. *Could this have been what the second puzzle piece was for? Am I supposed to pick one of these to live in now, or will I be pulled between them for the rest of my life?* Ian can't help but think this to himself.

No, Ian. You do not have to choose. You already know what's real and where you belong, Kenzie thinks these words to Ian.

I'm scared! How do I know what the right decision is? Are any of you in the other alternate world? Ian thinks back to Kenzie.

You already know the answers to those questions, Ian. You just have to make your decision final, she thinks back to him.

But I don't want to leave any of you. You are all so important to me. You are my friends, my family. My life will never be the same again, Ian replies.

Is that a bad thing, Ian? You have always been different, and you have had to overcome some hard battles in your life. When you go back, you will be more equipped to handle them and become a stronger person. We will forever be with you, Ian. We all love you, all the voices of Jax, Kenzie, Connor, Brayden, Chancellor Billie June, Garrett, Maclaine, Maria, Sebastian, Mason, and even Peter Hele, speak that last sentence together.

As Ian is sitting up in his bed, the one at the school, he has tears streaming down his face. He is crying uncontrollably and thinks back, *I love you all too. Please don't ever leave me. I am strongest only when we are all together.*

Once Ian finishes his thought to this team, he opens his eyes and realizes he is actually sitting in a bed in a hospital ICU. He is alone at the time he wakes up, but not for too long. As he wakes up, so do his monitors attached to his body. Once they begin to sound off, two nurses and three doctors enter his room. They all enter with precautions, as their previous interactions with Ian awake have not been pleasant.

To their surprise, Ian is fully awake and actually conscious of his surroundings and where he is. His eyes are swollen and still wet from his saying 'goodbye' to all his friends, but he knows he's going to be okay because one day he will see them all again. Ian believes they are all in the alternate timeline he did not choose. One day he can use the 'Time Keeper' to go back and make a different choice if he wants.

Ian's mother comes running into his room and gives him the biggest hug ever. She is so afraid to let him go, afraid she may lose him like so many other families have to this new virus, and she is not ready to risk that.

"Don't worry, mom. I'm going to be staying here this time for sure. Where is Kayla? Is she here and okay?" Ian asks his mother.

About that time, another nurse comes rushing into Ian's room demanding one of the three doctors in his room come with her, saying, "The girl is awake now. I'm not sure how, or why, but she just happened to wake up calling for 'Ian'," she finishes.

"Is her name Kayla?" Ian asks the nurse.

"I'm sorry, but I can't release that information to you."

"Yes, her name is Kayla," one of the doctors blurts out.

"When can I see her? I need to tell her we did it!" Ian exclaims.

"Relax, Ian. You will see her when you are both better. She has been in the hospital longer than you have. She will need rest and tests done on her. You understand, don't you?" Ian's mother asks. "Besides, I just got you back and don't want to risk losing you"

"Don't worry, mom. As I said before, I'm not going anywhere. For now anyway," Ian says with a smile of HOPE, like the hope that's still in Pandora's box.

THE
END

Epilogue: Alexis

Now that Travis has returned to the High Court's claiming he and his people, the Windairians, are able to go back and fix the small problems they have created. The small things, like the others of the High Courts have compromised, like when Fisher left a puzzle piece for Kayla to find. Another is when Emma gave Ian and Kenzie an extra forty-five minutes of time. And the worst one of all is when King Payton made it possible for Junior to gain access to Garrett's mind while he was awake. To Travis, this one most of all has the potential of creating the most damage. Especially if they find out who each other are.

"Now, we are still in the process of determining which of your 'Helpful Tasks' needs to be corrected first. So, we need a little time to calculate which ones will have the most alterations in the future, then we will proceed from there. Now, we will need to get with each of you, alone so you can tell us what your purpose was for your 'Help,' is that understood?" Travis finishes.

"We will need a room, separate from this one. It needs to be a room where each of the other High Court Members can feel free to speak the truth. Do you have a room like that, Councilman?" Travis asks.

"Yes, we have a room that is exactly like you are requesting," Councilman replies.

"Great. Can you or someone take us to this room, please?" Travis asks of the Councilman.

"Yes, of course. I will take to you the room myself," Council Leader assures Travis.

"Perfect, then let's get a move on. I hope it's not too far from where we are now," Travis replies to the Council Leader.

"It's not far from here at all. It's close enough for you to call each group in, one at a time and question them, and have the next group in the room only seconds after the previous group has been dismissed," the Council Leader says to Travis.

"That will be the perfect room that we will need to get through this process," Travis tells the Council Leader.

"Then, if you do not mind, follow me. The room is just down this hall," the Council Leader tells Travis and his group. As they approach the door to the new meeting room, the Council Leader turns the doorknob and swings the door open to the inside of the room.

The Council Leader wants Travis to see the interior of this room, for its size and accommodations, which he is hoping will suit them perfectly fine. "Well, what do you think of this room? Do you think it has enough to offer you as far as necessities, enough to complete your tasks? Because as far as privacy goes, this is the most secure room we have."

"If it is the most secure room you have to offer, then it will have to do. While we get settled in here, how about you go and let the others know we will be with them shortly?" Travis strongly suggests to the Council Leader.

With Travis' suggestion, the Council Leader nods his head and turns to begin his walk back down the hallway he had just guided them down from the others in the Grand Meeting room.

"So, who do you think we should start with first?" Travis asks the other Windairians. They traveled with him back to the Council's Headquarters after he had been dismissed so quickly earlier.

"I say we talk to Emma first. I want to find out what she really hoped to gain by giving Ian and Kenzie an extra forty-five minutes in time. I want to know how she was able to get them to agree to use the time to speak to Garrett again, instead of trying anything else," replies Adrienne. She is one of the Windairians who has been one of Travis' most trusted companions, who he trusts with his life to confront the High Court and Council Leader.

"Well, I was a bit more interested in finding out why Fisher would leave that puzzle piece for Kayla to find. I mean, really? What does, or can a puzzle piece do for our sake?" Rick says in rebuttal to Adrienne's choice. Rick is another Windairian who is more of a second in command when Travis and Adrienne are not around.

"And no one wants to know why King Payton had Garrett and Junior meet during this time period? They are from different times and places. Not to mention the most important connection they share, which thankfully has not been discovered, or revealed yet by either of them," asks Jessica, the last of the Windairians to travel back with the other three.

They all begin to discuss why their person should be the one to speak to first. The Council Leader has made his way back to the High Court's meeting room.

***

"So, why are you back here with us? We figured you would be staying with Travis and his people now that he is back and claims to be able to fix everything," Fisher asks the Council Leader upon his return to the group in the Grand Meeting room.

"Travis just asked me to find him a room, and that's what I did. I know they want to speak to each of us in private regarding the roles we played in assisting Kayla, Ian, and Kenzie in the past. They hope to be able to figure out exactly how they will be able to get back and repair what we have done," the Council Leader explains to Fisher and the rest of the High Court members.

"What do you mean, 'repair,' what we have done? We have not had enough time to see if any of what we achieved has worked. It takes time for the ripples to catch up to us to know for sure," Emma spits out with a defense of her actions.

"Now calm down, everyone. I think I would rather know sooner than later if what you all did works, instead of waiting to see if our present time changes for the worse. Wouldn't you all agree?" Council Leader reminds them all of what is at stake for them.

"Yes, I'm sure we would all agree with you, but their choice of word, 'repair,' already assumes that our work has and will fail. Now, how in the world would they know whether or not our plans have worked in the first place? They have not told us yet about what they can do or have already done in the past. How are we expected to trust someone who just may have gone back in time and set our plans on a path to fail so they can look like the heroes?" Fisher is asking for the entire High Court.

"Maybe he used a poor choice of words, or maybe you are taking it out of context. Have any of you thought that he is here for the same reasons you all stayed? He came back here because he is afraid and honestly wants to help? Remember, he and his people have just as much to lose as you all do if the timeline is not corrected. Let us hope you are all thinking about this when he does speak to you all. Because this is going to be the only way we all make it through this mess. We all will need to listen and ask questions, but most importantly, work together," the Council Leader finishes his speech with a sense of pride.

"So, how long do we have to wait to see who they want to target first?" Rose is asking in place of Emma this time.

"Travis did not give me a timeframe on when the interviews would begin. I would assume they will start soon, considering what little time we have left before the time ripples start to make their way up to us," the Council Leader responds to Rose and anyone else who may be listening.

The entire room remained silent after the Council Leader said what he felt needed to be said.

***

"Do you all mind stopping all of the arguing about who we should speak to first, please? I already know who we should question first, and that is the Council Leader. Not one of you has even suggested it to him. Have any of you wondered why any of this is happening in the first place? Do any of you want to know why they want us to go back and fix something that one of their people did in the past? Don't any of you want to know why their person would want to do what they did before we fix it? We need to rise above the others and make sure that we ask the right questions to the correct people and not be so power-hungry and petty. We do not want to lose sight of the big picture, do we? Now, do you all agree with me, or do we need to keep arguing?" Travis lays down his own theories to the group.

"No, I can say I have not thought of the Council Leader at all. I figured he is just the person responsible for getting every one of the leaders together," Rick answers Travis. 'Why would we ask HIM anything?"

"The fact is, he has been able to bring us all out of our homes, including Fisher, which none of us even knew about," Travis replies to Rick.

"Now that is a completely new way to go when you have nothing left to go for," Adrienne expresses to Travis.

"Excuse me? Do you believe that I am just making things up as I go? I'm sure if I had said we were going with your suggestion, you would not be questioning mine at this very moment," Travis questions Adrienne's motives for her observation.

"No, Sir, that is not what I am implying. I am simply curious as to why you would pick the least suspicious person to question first. I mean, he has done nothing to the past, and the other three Leaders have," Adrienne clarifies her poor choice of words.

"Sometimes, the least suspicious acts are the most obvious ones. One cannot keep their hands clean if they keep digging in the dirt all day, so they have others do their dirty work for them. That is what makes the Council Leader the most obvious person to speak to first, to find out what would make one of their own people do something this severe in history. The others are merely doing what the Council Leader has told them and doing things they think can help correct their people's mistakes. The Council Leader is using all of us to fix their problem that will affect us all. I, for one, want to know what they did to make someone never want to exist. Don't any of you wonder the same thing?" Travis explains in more detail to Adrienne and the other Windairians.

"Yes, that does sound logical, except one thing," Rick says to Travis.

"And what exactly would that be, if I may ask?"

"Wouldn't we want to speak to all of the other High Court leaders, plant this seed in their minds before we actually speak to the Council Leader? That would give us more people on our side. Right now, we could use everyone we can get on our side, don't you think? Also, there could be some important information we could gather from each of them that would help us put more pressure on the Council Leader," Rick finishes.

"I have to be honest with you, Rick, and say that is a great idea. Once we accuse the Council Leader to his face, then there will be no need to question the other leaders of the High Court, so we will not find out what they actually know about the Council or its leader. We do need to question the other first," Adrienne agrees with Rick.

"I can't believe the two of you can agree on anything at all these days. The time ripples must be doing its damage," Travis says jokingly to the pair of them.

"Very funny, Travis. Are you not pleased that we are at least halfway agreeing with your idea about the Council Leader?" Adrienne sarcastically replies to Travis.

"I'm just surprised you two would agree on anything, even if it is just against me," Travis details.

"Well? What do you think of what Rick said? Would it be better to go after the Council Leader first or last?" Adrienne asks Travis for his opinion.

"I think that is a perfect idea. Now you know why I chose you all to come with me back here. You all can see a grander picture than just me or even the Council or even the High Court leaders for that matter," Travis expressed to his team of Windairians that have come back with him to the Council meeting place.

"So, how do you suggest we approach this situation? Do you think we should be direct with the other High Court leaders, or do we beat around the bush with them to keep them just talking? That way, we can get as much information from them as possible, without them suspecting what we are trying to get from them," Adrienne asks Travis.

"I am open to hearing what everyone thinks we should do on this matter. I know we can come up with a perfect solution if we all work together. That is the reason I chose each of you for this mission. You all offer different points of view and reasonings, but you all also never look away from a better solution than you own."

***

Alexis comes barging in through the High Court's chamber doors. All of the members stop and just stare at her, Fisher, Emma, Payton, and even the Council Leader.

"What are you doing here? You are supposed to be who we are looking to bring back to our timeline," the Council Leader asks.

"I am here because I had hoped that my son would follow me and never give up on the future we were supposed to have. Once he found out that our future and past had already been changed, he brought it to my attention. One of the best things about my son, Garrett Jr., is that, with the gift he already has from my family bloodline and the gifts from his father, he has abilities none of us could ever foresee. Now my only question is, why did King Preston want to ruin it all by having them meet?" Alexis askes the High Court.

"I am not sure what you are referring to, Alexis, is it? My brother would have no reason to want you or your son out of the past or future. He does not know who your son's father is," King Payton explains.

"Then what do you say we bring King Preston back and ask him ourselves?" Alexis says as she calls in her son, Garrett Jr.

Before Junior can make it to Alexis, Travis and the other Windairian's walk into the chamber.

"What is all this commotion about?" Travis demands to know.

"This is Alexis. She is the person we were trying to bring back to our timeline, and it seems that what we did worked. So, in reality, your services are no longer needed.

"Now, can we get back to how do you plan on bringing back my brother, King Preston?" King Payton asks Alexis.

"Junior, would you like to do the honors?" Alexis asks her son.

"You bet I would," Junior says with a smile as he closes his eyes and thinks hard about King Preston, and poof, there stands the King.

"How did you do that? That's not even possible. If it were, you could have saved us all a lot of trouble and time by just bringing your mother back," Prince Payton announces to Junior for everyone to hear.

"It's best that you do not worry about that right now, Prince Payton. It will soon all come out," Alexis lets him know.

"Now, King Preston, now that we have you back, do you know what happened to you?" Alexis askes.

"No, I remember being here one minute and gone the next, then now I am back again. What has been going on?"

"Let's start with the fact that Junior uncovered that your brother, Prince Payton, has been working with a man named Chad. Chad is not from this world, and let's say not a very nice person to Junior's father, Garrett. He asked Chad to go back in time to make sure that Junior was never born. For him to do that, he made it possible for Junior to meet his father way before their time, which could have ended up leaving him gone forever. This would have ensured the Prince would remain the King of the Embers forever.

"That is the person that had been helping Mason all along, with the guidance of the Prince here.

"You did what? You had me erased from History with a time ripple so you could become King of the Embers? Why would you do something like that?" King Preston asks his little brother.

"Because I am tired of being in your shadow all the time. Also, because you were becoming weak. You have not wanted to start a war in so many years, and our people are getting restless. They need a leader who can take us to victory over these other people. That's also why we needed the Council Leader's help getting all the group leaders together. We had heard rumors of the Aquarians, but they were just rumors, but now we know they are true, we know how we can defeat them," Prince Payton replies.

"Excuse me? I have no idea what he is talking about. I had no part of this scheme of the Prince's. I just did what I thought was necessary to save history," the Council Leader speaks in his defense.

"Please, sir, we have already determined you had to be complicit in whatever was going on. We just didn't know to what extent. Now we know," Travis offers up the evidence they have.

"Well, Prince Payton, your plans have all been defeated, and now the future Junior is seeing is an amazing one, just one without you in it," Alexis says while looking over at King Preston.

"I can't believe you would go through all of this just to start wars, brother. But it is time you learn your lesson about messing with the powers greater than yours. You will no longer be part of our Royal Family. You will for now on be a prisoner of the Aquarians, if Fisher approves, since it was his people you were trying to oust," King Preston offers up his brother to Fisher and the Aquarians for safekeeping.

"It would be our pleasure to house your brother as a sign of peace between our two tribes. But who will get the Council Leader?" Fisher wonders out loud.

"I believe we will take him with us since it was us that figured out he was part of this plot in some way or another and was just about to expose him because Alexis and her son showed up," Travis of the Windairians offers.

"That all sounds perfect to me," Alexis protests. "How do the rest of you feel about this?"

"We are all in agreement with you, Alexis, and also would like to make you the new Council Leader. For you and your son's sacrifices to save history and bring an end to this unforeseen traitor among us. If you would accept the position, that is," Emma answers for the rest of the High Court.

"I would love to, and things will be different now. We will all work as a team to ensure our nothing like this will ever happen again. Thank you all for the help you gave us along the way. And even though Junior's father is not here, I would like to give thanks to him for providing the second puzzle piece, the one that kept Ian in our timeline, which is now in our future."

"Here, here, Garrett, Sr." they all chant.

Three Days Later

Once Kayla and Ian were healthy enough to leave the hospital, which was only three days after they both woke up, they went home. Upon making it home to his Brooklyn apartment with his mother, Ian notices a familiar face looking as if it is moving into their building.

As Ian approaches this new tenant, and she turns around, he sees Maria.

"Maria? Is this really you?" Ian shouts with enthusiasm.

"Um, yes. That is my name, but how do you know that? Have we met before?" Maria asks back with a confused look upon her face.

"Ian, I see you have met Maria. I told you about her. Maria is moving here from Texas. These are her niece and nephew, Kenzie and Connor. They will be here helping Maria move in and even on weekends and holidays. Everyone, this is my best friend Ian I told you about," Kayla surprises Ian as she is walking out of the entrance of their apartment building with a mask on, with Kenzie and Connor, both wearing masks as well, due to the pandemic.

"Well, it's nice to meet you all. I hope we get to see more of each other after this pandemic is over when we can finally stop wearing these facemasks and staying at least six feet apart. After everyone has completed their quarantine since you just got to town, maybe we all could get to know each other more," Ian suggests.

"That sounds amazing, Ian. We are on the third floor. Once we are out of quarantine, I believe it should be about fourteen days here in Brooklyn, we will get ahold of Kayla and set something up," Maria states, while Kenzie and Connor both cheer.

"Until then. I'm sorry we are unable to help you move right now, but if we could, we would, for sure," Kayla says as she and Ian walk away.

"I have a good feeling about them, don't you, Ian?" Kayla asks.

"I do. And you never told me about them. Are they who I think they are?" Ian calls Kayla out for telling a lie.

"How would I know what you are thinking? It's not like I can read your mind. You must still be dealing with the 'brain fog' from the virus," Kayla replies with a hidden smile on her face.

***

Now that many of the schools have gone to online teaching, Ian is surprised to see he has a new History teacher and teacher's aide.

"Let me guess. You already told me about the school changes with Jax and Brayden being our new teachers?" Ian types a private message to Kayla in their virtual classroom before the new teachers could introduce themselves to the class.

"Yes, see, your 'brain fog' is already clearing up," Kayla laughs out loud from her bedroom, where she is attending her video classes for the day, so no one can hear her laughing.

"Hello class, my name is Jax, which is short for Jaxon, and the other young fellow you see here is my teacher's assistant, Brayden. We will be your new History teachers for this year. If you need anything, just let one of us know, and we will help you. Now, this is very important. Some weeks we will have class via video, and some weeks we will be in the actual classroom here at the school. So keep up with the school schedule.

"Now, if at any time you feel sick during a workweek when you are required to be at school, just let one of us know and stay home. We will include you in the class while you are sick via video, so you do not miss anything. While learning at home may be hard for some of you, either you don't have a computer or are unable to learn by yourself, we are here to help. If you need a computer, we will provide one for you. If you need additional help on an assignment, Brayden is here to help tutor anyone who needs it, either one on one by video or in person at the school with facemasks and social distances, but only if you are not feeling sick for the in-person tutoring.

"Does everyone understand the rules of in-person learning and in-home learning?" Jax asks his new class, which includes Kayla and Ian.

"Yes, sir. And welcome to Brooklyn," Ian answers for the class.

***

The very next week is Kayla and Ian's first day back at public, in-person school. Ian is not as thrilled as Kayla is about being back. But he knows he only has this one last year before he graduates.

"So, how are things going with you and River Kate? How is that long-distance relationship going? And how did you two meet again?" Kayla asks Ian.

"We met online. She accidentally sent a message to me when she was trying to send one to a friend of hers here in Brooklyn, and we just started talking from there. Speaking of long-distance relationships, how are yours and Garrett's? Where did you say he lived again, Hawaii?" Ian replies.

"Well played, Ian, well played. Is that a security guard at our school?" Kayla inquires of a person she notices in the crowd in a uniform.

"Well, why don't we go and find out," Ian says to Kayla.

They both walk over to the security guard, and as they get closer, Ian notices it is Maclaine.

"You have not told me about Maclaine working here now," Ian says to Kayla.

"Who's Maclaine?"

"Fine, play like you don't know what's going on here," Ian replies with a giggle.

"I have no clue on who this person is, and how do you know his name?" Kayla asks Ian.

Ian does not answer but walks up to the security guard and starts speaking to him.

"Good morning, My name is Ian, and this is Kayla. We are both Seniors this year. We have never had a security guard here before, so why have they hired one this year?" Ian questions the guard.

"Well, it's nice to meet you both. My name is Maclaine. I have been hired to help control the bullying problem here at this school. It was brought to the attention of the School Board of several incidents in the past few years, and I am here to make sure that stops. But don't worry, I am not the only one here. There are plenty of others that volunteer to help watch these halls during school weeks. This way, you all can enjoy school," Maclaine replies with a smile.

"We are very glad to have you here with us, Maclaine. It would not feel like home unless we were all together, watching out for each other, as we should," Ian says to Maclaine as he and Kayla walk away to their first class, not giving the security guard time to reply. Ian feels he understands anyway.

***

Mason had taken his final hour very seriously. He came to the conclusion that he must learn how to accept the loss of his family. He thought of ways he could make their lives mean something, no matter how long or short they were.

Once Mason is able to accept those things about his mother, brother, and sister, he flashes out of the room at the Believer's Headquarters to an office in New York City. Unsure if it is his office, as he has never seen this room before, he begins to walk around the modest desk to look at the pictures that are upon it. The photos almost give Mason a heart attack.

Mason looks hard at the photos. His desk is filled with photos of him, a wife and two small children. Every photo is filled with friends, family, smiles, tears, and laughter. Just as he was promised, everything was exactly the way it was meant to be.

Acknowledgements

I would like to thank family and friends for allowing me to use their names for my characters. As a first-time series author, it was easier for me to remember names this way. My family members are Chancellor Billie June (my Grandmother), Donna (my mother), Marty (my uncle), John Dock and Jessica (little brother and sister-in-law), Jaxson and Kenzie (John Dock and Jessica's children, my nephew and niece), Pete (big brother), Kayla and Kourtney (Pete's daughters, my nieces), Ashley (little sister), Brayden (Ashley's son, my nephew), Tracy and Michael (cousins), Jennifer (cousin), Fisher and Alexis (Jennifer's son and daughter, my cousins), Stephanie (cousin), Travis, Preston, Payton (Stephanie's son's, my cousins), Jon (cousin), Jerry and Delores (aunt and uncle) Brian, Connor and Emma (my editor, Patricia Carpenter with Carpenter Editing Services LLC, son, and grandchildren), Carol and Pam (close friends from Overtime Grill and Bar, Birmingham, AL), Tori and Jacob for allowing me to use their baby River Kate's name (close friends from Birmingham, AL). I would also like to thank the families that allowed me to include their loved ones taken away from life too soon. They will now forever be characters in "Saving History Series," so, thank you Joseph 'Garrett', 'Clint', and 'Maclaine', and your families for sharing your lives with me. I hope I did right by them for you.

Next, I would like to thank my editor, Patricia, of Carpenter Editing Services, LLC. She has been a second mother to me for many years and with her editing skills, advice, and opinions on *Time Keeper, School Bound, Search Begins, Loose Ends,* and now *Final Hour*. Without her, this work of art would not be what it is today. She brings such joy to my writing with her suggestions and honest critiques. Not to mention, her patience with me has been amazing. With my reading disability, she has been able to teach me more about proper English and being able to become a better writer. I feel that I have grown so much as an author with fewer mistakes due to her teaching. If I could nominate her for a Teacher of the Year award, I would.

I need to thank my Beta Reader, Bernadette Horgan, who has been able to give me great feedback, honestly, even if she thought it was tough, she gave it because it made my stories better. You can follow her on Instagram @bibliophile1996, if you want to send her something to read and leave amazing reviews for you. Thank you all.

I would also like to give a quick thank you to the places that allowed me to sit and write in their establishments when I needed that creative energy. A few of those places are Overtime Grill and Bar (off Lakeshore Pkwy in Birmingham, AL), Dunkin Donuts (off HWY 119 in Pelham, AL), Tejano's Tex-Mex (Cooper, TX), Bada Bing's Atlanta (Atlanta, GA), Pencil Factory Shops & Flats

(Atlanta, GA), DoubleTree Hotel (Chattanooga Downtown, TN), Blakes (Atlanta, GA), Friends on Ponce (Atlanta, GA), and Barns & Noble Edgewood (Atlanta, GA), Midtown Moon, Felix's, Hideaway, and Oscars (Midtown Atlanta), BJ Roosters (Atlanta) Piedmont Park Atlanta, Lazy Llama (Midtown Atlanta), The Rail (Commerce, TX), Chili's (Sulphur Springs, TX). Without these places listed, I would have been lost. As someone with ASD, social settings are not easy for me, and I never felt out of place or any pressure at these creative energy spots. These places made me feel at home every time.

Last, but not least, I want to thank my fans. If not for you, my words would sit on paper, never to be read.

About the Author

Robert Starnes is not only the author of the *Multifamily Housing Guide Series: Leasing 101 - Garden Style*, and the Saving History Series: *Time Keeper, School Bound, Search Begins, Loose Ends*, and now *Final Hour*, but he is also the publisher. He created Starnes Books LLC so that he could have full control over his work and to be able to help other unpublished authors with free advice on what they can do to save money and not be taken advantage of for their hard work.

After being diagnosed with Asperger's Syndrome, which is now part of a broader category called ASD (Autism Spectrum Disorder), at the age of 43, things started to click with him. After identifying and managing his ASD, Robert was able to hone in on his creative writing. When he was younger, he did not like to read because he had difficulty with the words on the pages in front of him. Robert knew the words and understood them, but his brain would comprehend them faster than his voice could speak them. That caused him to either leave out words or to read very slowly so that he could have his eyes go back over the words again two to three times before his voice caught up with his brain. This embarrassment would stop him from reading for many years.

As an adult learning to face his fears, he began to read John Grisham novels. He loves the law and movies, so it was perfect for him to read "The Last Juror" before watching the movie. After reading such a great novel then watching the movie, Robert quickly learned he enjoyed comparing the differences between novels and the movies that were made from them. That was all it took for him to begin to enjoy reading for the first time. For many years, he would only read novels that were going to become movies. Then he read another novel that became a movie, but they never finished the movie series. The novel was so good that he ended up reading the entire book series. That gave him a new enjoyment for reading without the novels becoming movies.

With this in Robert's mind, he has written his series for anyone that may be going through the same things he went through. He is trying to find a way for them to connect with the world of reading. He believes that anyone can read and write a perfectly great action-packed novel, and it does not have to be 800 pages thick to be accomplished. He believes giving someone the opportunity and a way to enter the world of reading, that's the accomplishment. No one should be afraid to read or write in their own style for others to be able to want to read. His mind does not work the same as a traditional writer's does. His mind retains things much more than another person's may, so you will not find very much repeating or recapping in his series. You will find action, adventure, and history from the very first chapter to the very end.

Robert believes that everyone is different and unique and should be celebrated every day for being just who they are. He finds that when life may get you down, you can always get away in your own imagination with the help of a good book.

He was born in Texas but now does most of his writing in Alabama, Georgia, and Texas. To learn more about him and his books, visit starnesbooksllc.com, @starnesbooksllc on Instagram, @Starnes_Books on Twitter facebook.com/savinghistoryseries.

Robert Starnes

Books by Robert Starnes

Saving History Series

Time Keeper – Starnes Books LLC (2018)
School Bound – Starnes Books LLC (2019)
Search Begins – Starnes Books LLC (2019)
Loose Ends – Starnes Books LLC (2019)
Final Hour – Starnes Books LLC (2021)

The Multifamily Housing Guide Series

Leasing 101: Garden Style – Starnes Books, LLC (2018)

The Multifamily Housing Guide – Leasing 101 Garden Style Edition – Lulu's publishing (2016 retired print)

Books Published by Starnes Books LLC

***Novel Study – Time Keeper** – Patricia Carpenter (2018)*
***Trip of a Lifetime** – Eric K. Reinholt (2020)*

www.ingramcontent.com/pod-product-compliance
Lightning Source LLC
Chambersburg PA
CBHW050250110726